R. M. KROGMAN

MARKED

A DARK FANTASY
～NOVELLA～

DRAGONKEEPER PRESS

ACKNOWLEDGMENTS

Many thanks to my beta readers J. DeBoer, H. Dunwall, K. Kanyaya, K. Krogman, B. Martin, E. McDermott, and C. Sciriha for their time and comments. Your enthusiasm and critical feedback are both essential to making this the best story it can be. Thank you to B. Willis for your continual encouragement.

A Note to Readers

Curses are powerful, if you believe in them enough.

Marked tells the story of a side character that you'll see again in the epic fantasy *The Keepers of Midgate*. This story is best read first, but can be read as a stand-alone story. Come with me to Midgate. Enter this beautiful, mountainous landscape with dragons on the peaks and threats hidden in the valley shadows. Meet Davon, a simple boy with a simple life. Cry with him, endure with him, and stay with him when others don't.

Welcome to Midgate, a world where curses and blessings may be real. Be warned, a society ruled by fear is a society of judgment. A close-knit community can be closed. And innocence can hardly endure when the world is so corrupted by greed, selfishness, and impatience. Content warnings include: physical violence, trauma, child abuse/neglect, and suicide. If you have any concerns, contact the author at https://rmkrogman.com under **Contact**.

1

SUMMERTIME WAS THE BEST part of living in the high meadows of Mirat's mountains. The sunshine made the glaciers glitter on the peaks above, and the late flowers bloomed, attracting tiny butterflies that moved in clustered groups.

One landed on Davy's nose, and another landed on his forehead. Two more fluttered on his arm, touching him with delicate curled tongues as they explored the sweat and salt on his skin. He suppressed a giggle, not wanting to startle them away, and lay frozen by the clear, cool stream that meandered through the valley.

His father called to him.

"I can't move, Pa," he answered through his teeth. He crossed his eyes trying to focus on the butterfly tickling his nose. It slowly flapped its orange patterned wings as it kissed him.

His father appeared in his peripheral vision, using his crook to step carefully along the bank. Sheep ambled alongside him and through the stream, lapping the fresh water as they went.

"Looks like we may have to stay here for a while then." Pa smiled.

Davy lay in the grass for a while longer, examining the cloud shapes in the bright blue sky. Some of them were fantastic shapes—pirate ships chased by myr warriors, waving banners, knights on horses, and dragons—but most of them looked like sheep. Fluffy and white like the flock, although their sheep had dark faces and skin beneath the poof of white.

"It's past time for shearing again," muttered Pa. He stared at the clouds too. "Spring flies by at the speed of a charging horse."

"Or a ghastwolf," Davy agreed, seeing that shape in the sky, its legs shifting in a nebulous trot.

His father gave him a sharp glance. "Don't say that, son. It's bad luck." Then his face softened, and he patted Davy's arm.

It frightened the butterflies away.

Davy sat up with a disappointed sigh as the orange and violet wings retreated further upstream.

Shearing was a chore, but it wasn't nearly as bad as what came after. Treating and beating the wool for the spinster in town was far less fun. Davy would help Ma and Pa as he always did, and then they would go to town to sell. He had helped prepare the wool for four or five seasons now, after he had gotten big enough to follow instructions.

"Will the ol'Campens come over?" he asked hopefully.

Pa nodded. "They will, just as we helped them earlier this year."

Davy brightened at the thought of Tara and Mikkel, the daughter and son of Mr. and Mrs. ol'Campen. Mikkel was tall and strong; he even knew how to use a bow and set traps. Tara, who was only a few years older than Davy, was smart; she knew all the plants and berries in the valley and how to use them. She even claimed to know a few green magika remedies like the Herbsman in town did, which Davy thought was very impressive.

He stared after the flitting butterflies for a few more moments, then stood and whistled for one of the dogs. He made his way to the other side of the flock, following Pa's hand signals as they gathered the wanderers into a tighter group. They herded the flock down the valley toward the house as the sun dropped lower.

"Want me to bring you supper, Pa?"

Pa nodded again. He would stay out with the dogs and sheep all night.

Davy skipped down to the house, a small stone and log cottage tucked amongst the pines at the edge of the meadow.

Ma stood in the doorway waiting for him with a smile. "Get in here, boy, before the dragons come out." She lightly smacked his rear as he went through the door.

"It's not that late, Ma." He giggled, then reported Pa's need for supper.

Ma hummed and bustled over to the cookpot. She ladled a watery rabbit stew into a bowl and handed it to him. "Hurry back now. It's getting darker by the minute."

"Can I stay out with Pa?"

"Not tonight. I need help sharpening shears." She waved one of the dull tools at him and ushered him out.

Davy delivered the stew and walked back slowly. The jagged Sikrat Mountains already cast long shadows over the valley in places, and he could see the silhouettes of a few dragons far above. On a distant craggy peak, one stretched its wings wide, absorbing the heat of the sinking sun. It shone a burnished orange, light streaming through its thin wing membranes. The dragons always perched high at dusk, seeming to bid farewell to the sun.

Davy wondered if they were like lizards, cold-blooded and needing sun for their body heat. They seemed kind of lizard-like, at least from far away. He had never seen one of the predators closer, and Pa said that was a good thing.

Who knew how much damage a single dragon could cause their flock?

Pa didn't like talking about it either, because talking about predators could bring bad luck and call them in. Everyone knew that. Davy's mention of a ghastwolf earlier was foolish, and he regretted not saying something else, like a myrmaiden or a robed Temple mage summoning a ball of fire with his hands. At least Davy hadn't said what he really saw, which was a trotting ghastwolf snapping at the fluffy tail of a cloud sheep. That would really have upset Pa.

By the time he re-entered the cottage, it too had fallen under the creeping shadow of dusk, and Ma lit a candle for their evening work.

He yawned. "Can we do it tomorrow?"

"We need to be ready to shear tomorrow," Ma replied, handing him a pair of worn shears and a sharpening stone. "Always work hard, Davy, and you'll earn a good living and respect from others. That's how life works."

The ol'Campens arrived early the next morning. Tara skipped up the narrow track ahead of her brother Mikkel and her mother, pausing occasionally to smell the tiniest of flowers as she passed. She waved at Davy as soon as she saw him in the meadow, and he waved back with both arms flung wide. Mikkel slowly raised his arm as well.

Like Pa, Mr. ol'Campen remained with his own flock at all times, but his family provided welcome assistance as they sheared. Mrs. ol'Campen had even brought a basketful of sweet biscuits drizzled with fragrant kiltflower honey. (That had to be an invention of Tara's.)

Mikkel, being the strongest besides Pa, was one of the holders, securing each animal with a calm, confident grip as the women clipped off heavy mats of wool. Tara and Davy scurried back and forth, taking the clumps and setting them in a pile in the small stable, just to one side of the horse's stall.

Davy hefted a large mat with a grunt. Ma had managed to shear the entire sheep nearly clean in one piece, and the thick wool was heavy enough to make him stagger.

Tara giggled. "Slow down, Davy." She gathered wool in her own arms and hurried after him toward the stable. "I can hardly keep up with you."

Davy laughed and sped up over the familiar meadow terrain. "The sooner we finish, the sooner we can eat biscuits!" he declared.

He heard Tara behind him, laughing as she ran, but then she yelped. He turned to see her stumbling in the meadow, and he dropped his wool to hurry back.

"Are you okay? There's a rock there, sorry."

Tara rubbed her knee with a wistful smile. "I didn't see it. Ouch." She wrinkled her nose, then glanced at the pile of wool she had dropped in the grass. Her face lit up, and she pointed at a slender-stalked grass with a cluster of yellow star-shaped flowers on its head. "Hey, that's mountain corn flower. The Herbsman in town says it's good for stomachaches."

Davy offered a hand up, which she ignored.

She peered more closely at the flower. "But, he also said that it looks like a different one that makes you throw up, so you really have to pay attention to the shape of the flowers."

Davy glanced up at Ma, who was nearly half-done shearing another sheep. She met his gaze and frowned. Davy beckoned at Tara. "Come on, we need to keep working."

Tara waved her hand at him and put her nose to the corn flower. "My knee still hurts. Besides, we're not in that big of a hurry. Today is supposed to be fun."

"Ma said it's supposed to be hard work," Davy countered, feeling nervous down in his gut. "Ma said hard work is the way you earn your keep." He began to pick up the scattered scraps of wool Tara had dropped, so he could pile them all back in her arms when she was ready.

"Hard work is great, Davy, but you don't have to earn anything with those who care about you.

They'll care about you anyway, no matter what." She grinned as she took the pile of wool from him. "You're going to get sweet biscuits when we're done, even if you catch your breath for a minute right now. I made the honey syrup myself."

Davy led her with a hurried step toward the stable, grabbing his own wool on the way. "Did you make the biscuits too?"

"I helped Mama." She stepped more carefully, favoring her sore knee and scanning the ground ahead of her.

"I wish I knew how to do that. Ma would appreciate that," Davy thought aloud. He wished Tara would move a little faster. A glance back at the group shearing confirmed that they were behind, and Ma gave him a stern look. He dumped the wool as quickly as he could and started to run back.

"Don't step on the corn flower," Tara called.

"Why?"

"I might need it if you eat too many biscuits." Her clear laughter rang out from behind him, and he rolled his eyes. She was probably right.

As Davy recalled from helping for several seasons in a row, what followed shearing was less fun. The ol'Campens returned home to their own work, leaving his family to beat and treat the wool for sale.

The process reeked of the horse and sheep urine used to break down the oil barrier on the wool. The wool had to be cleaned of debris and mud, treated, and beaten to flat mats of a uniform size and texture. Ms. ol'Lannery, the spinster in town, would evaluate their quality and pay them accordingly with the largest income they would have for the entire year. Davy was thorough on each and every step, gaining proud pats on the back and warm smiles from both Ma and Pa.

Whenever he could, he also relieved Pa in the fields, giving his father rest during the daylight. Daytime was safe enough, and it was the middle of summer. Pa had told Davy that ghastwolves usually moved higher and deeper into the mountains during summer, and that they didn't seem to like the light. Dragons didn't move to a different territory throughout the year, but they never hunted during the day. Despite their size and vicious appearance, they tended to shy away from human habitation, making the flock much safer. Davy could cover the daylight hours alone, his back arched with pride and his hand clutching Pa's crook.

When the wool was finally ready for sale, Pa helped them load it all into their cart, stacking the mats as high as possible and strapping them down with rope. Ma clambered onto the driver's seat, and Pa handed her the reins, hanging on for an extra moment as they bade farewell. As usual, he would remain with the flock, guarding them with his crook and dogs while Ma took care of bartering in town.

Davy licked his lips. A trip to town meant the possibility of a sticky sweetbun, or maybe a hard candy.

Ma clicked her tongue at the horse, and the wagon creaked forward on the rough, pitted track that led from their home to the distant town down the mountain. She blushed as Pa winked at her and waved.

Davy waved back enthusiastically, his mind still lingering on the concentrated sweetness of his possible reward, and he resolved to work very hard helping Ma do business in town.

They bounced their way to town, passing the ol'Campens and a few other farmsteads with equally quaint cottages and similar livestock, and eventually reaching the spinster's home.

Ms. ol'Lannery lived on the edge of town in a larger house with an enclosed animal yard. Davy considered that a sign of her wealth, for she could gather her flock up in a safe place and not struggle to watch them during the winter. The fields adjacent belonged to her too, and her own smaller flock grazed contentedly. Her sheep were white as snow, their floppy ears hanging comically on either side of bright faces, a contrast to their own flock. Davy knew Ms. ol'Lannery needed the volume of wool for spinning and even hired men since she had never married, and again he marveled at her wealth. She could probably buy sweetrolls whenever she wanted.

The door opened, revealing the more elderly woman. She beamed at them without showing her teeth, which emphasized the crowsfeet at the corners of her eyes and the lines on her cheeks.

"Mrs. ol'Sheffed, how lovely to see you, and you as well, Davy." She scruffed Davy's hair and welcomed them in, launching immediately into gossip.

Davy sat on a stool and kicked his legs as Ma and the spinster made polite conversation, then shifted to light bartering, then back again.

"The summer nights are beautiful, but praise the Light they're short," Ma said.

Ms. ol'Lannery made a plaintive sound of agreement in her throat and nodded knowingly. "Food aplenty, and yet the predators still harass the flocks, don't they? Seems the young ghastwolves split off from their parents this time of year, and of course the dragons are always hovering for a meal." She spit to one side for good luck, then leaned in with an over-loud whisper that obviously carried. "Did you hear, the family that just settled in that high valley—yes, that one—lost a goodly number of their sheep."

"To dragons?" Davy leaned forward, his interest piqued.

Ms. ol'Lannery pursed her lips, then spat to the side again.

Davy cringed, realizing his loud repetition of "dragons" was more bad luck, just like his mention of ghastwolves. He should have whispered. He spat to one side as well.

Ms. ol'Lannery nodded her approval, then continued. "Hard to say but they lost enough animals, they abandoned the half-built cottage and moved into town. Not sure they'll even attempt to restore the flock, or simply sell it to those with better luck in their stars. You know, I heard they set the cottage foundation stone without a blessing, they were in such a rush to settle. No wayfarers had passed through town recently, and they refused to wait."

"They could have bought one from the Herbsman on the other side of town," Ma declared with horror.

Ms. ol'Lannery shrugged her shoulders. "Serves them right, really, if they're willing to discard all luck for the sake of speed. They should have been more careful. Praise the Light they didn't lose more than a few sheep. I hear they have two lovely daughters, one blonde and one dark, would you believe it. A poor dowry they may have now, if the family can't recover."

Ma shuddered. "Thank I'ya we haven't faced such a dire situation."

Ms. ol'Lannery shook herself out of an exaggerated dark expression and sniffed loudly. "And may you never, Mrs. ol'Sheffed. Your sheep are the best in the district, nice quality wool, very unique texture and shade. I don't know how you've bred such a unique line, but I can always tell the quality when I pull the cards out. Perhaps you ought to buy a blessing from the next wayfarer that comes through town. I saw one pass by yesterday, and I believe they stopped for the night."

Ma patted Davy's shoulder. "We have good wool because we have good help cleaning and sorting," she said affectionately. (Davy straightened at that, making the stool creak.) "You know the ol' Sheffeds have a long history in the area, breeding that line from old blood."

Ms. ol'Lannery nodded. "Davy here could easily become a Herdsman, just as your husband could have been. I know *his* uncle went to Callendera for training."

"No money to enter the guild, unfortunately," replied Ma with a tinge of sadness. She shook Davy's shoulder, and he looked up at her blankly.

He didn't want to be shipped off to a guildhall somewhere. The Herding Master Hall was somewhere very far away to the south in a kingdom called Callendera, which sounded frightening and lonely. He was perfectly content helping Pa raise sheep in the valley with the majestic Sikrat Mountains watching over him.

Ms. ol'Lannery slapped her knees and stood. "Well that's a shame. Davy here would look fine in a green tunic with teal buttons. I suppose let's get you a little coin for your labor. Davy, jump into the cart, would you?" She continued chattering as they moved outside, speaking of the baker's growing son and the upcoming summer equinox celebration and the poor quality tools being made by a new smithy on the other side of town. A babe had been born last week, inspected thoroughly and found to have a suspicious-looking mark on its foot.

"Midwife nearly ended it then and there," Ms. ol'Lannery declared, "as it must be. Can't have a babe with the Mark of Evil on it. What terrible bad luck that'd bring! But the father insisted they call on the Temple for verification. Insisted! Can you imagine arguing with the midwife? She's seen plenty of babes. But send for a mage she did, and the mage decided the birthmark was just that, a birthmark and nothing more. Would you believe it?" She paused, waiting for Ma's astonished reaction to the shocking story before going on about what she had heard the mark looked like.

Davy scrambled up the back of the cart with a little help from Ma, and they unloaded the woolen mats as quickly as they could. Ms. ol'Lannery count-ed a number of coins into Ma's hand, and Davy thought he identified quarter-marks and half-marks amongst the pennies. He marveled at the amount of income going into Ma's leather purse; it was enough he couldn't add it all together. The two women curtsied politely to each other, and he and Ma headed further into town.

She seemed a little quiet, chewing on her lip as she guided the horse onward. Then again, maybe she seemed quiet because Ms. ol'Lannery was so chatty.

"I can smell the bakery from here," murmured Davy, thinking of the pile of coins weighing Ma's purse down. He looked up at Ma, his eyebrows raised in question.

She shook herself from her apparent reflections and kissed his forehead, then pressed a quarter-penny into his hand. "You've been very helpful today, son. Pick anything you want."

He chose a sticky roll smothered in sweet caramel, and he busied himself licking his fingers clean while Ma finished a few other tasks. She used some of their gains to get milled flour and leavening, a sackful of apples, and a barrel of ale. The brawny tavernkeeper loaded the barrel himself, giving Davy a wink and a smile for the business, and Davy grinned back with caramel stuck in his teeth.

Ma also bought a magical blessing from the wayfaring wagon parked near the tavern. Davy's mouth dropped open when he saw an entire penny exchanged for it. Good luck was worth it, he supposed, if it was real.

With a start, he realized Ma was probably buying it because of his foolish exclamation about predators, and he clamped his mouth shut. A whole penny wasted because of him? He would have apologized, but bringing it up again was probably worse.

Then they stopped at the smithy to get the horse re-shoed. Davy watched the blacksmith work, his fingers completely clean and his sticky roll gone. Ma chatted with the smith's wife while the man worked, but Davy followed on the man's heels, brimming with curiosity. The smith's shop featured mostly normal tools, a sharpening stone, and a forge, but it also had a few signs of black magika, the minor magika of metallurgy. The smith's wife practiced it, using the shavings and powders from her husband's business to create potions for stomach illness and other ailments. According to Ms. ol'Lannery, she had apprenticed to the Herbsman years ago.

Like the wayfarer's blessings, Davy wondered if the shiny green and orange powders really worked.

The smith pried each shoe off and cleaned each foot, scraping out dried muck and pebbles and extra growth. Then he tacked the new shoes on, patting the horse's shoulder afterward and mumbling a litany of words under his breath.

"Did you know we used to have a different horse?" Davy asked.

The smith grunted. "I remember."

"She came up lame, and Pa sold her to the butcher."

The smith grunted again and spat to one side. "It happens, boy, but you shouldn't mention that while shoeing another horse. Could hurt your trip home." He beckoned to his wife, who disappeared inside and re-appeared with a small jar of red dust. She sprinkled some over the horse's last foot, and the smith sighed. "No charge, just a bit of luck for the road."

When they climbed back onto the cart, Ma handed Davy the reins. He took them with reverence and wide eyes.

"Really? I can drive home?" He brightened at the thought.

Ma nodded. "Take her down this street and turn around, then easy through the town."

He straightened his shoulders and raised his chin as they passed by the smithy in the other direction, then the tavern, hoping both men noticed him driving their one-horse cart. They did, each of them grinning wide and waving. The tavernkeeper even tipped his cap as if Davy were an adult.

Pa would be proud when he saw them returning on the small track, cart laden with goods and his son driving.

2

ANOTHER CLEAR NIGHT BLESSED their valley, and a pleasant warm breeze blew down the eastern face to tickle their cheeks. The blanket of stars shone so brightly, it outlined the jagged silhouette of the Sikrat Range from behind and made the stony peaks seem darker. The quick moon was new, allowing the stars to shine all the brighter, and the slow moon had not yet risen.

Davy peered into the night, his haunches settled on a good rock and his father's crook in his hand. Pa leaned against the same rock, his head lolling onto Davy's lap and his arms crossed over themselves. He snored lightly.

Pa never did get much rest, even when Davy helped. That was part of keeping a flock, but Davy didn't mind too much. He grasped the crook entrusted to him more tightly and peered across the dark meadow. The flock slept soundly, and the dog whimpered as it chased rabbits in its dreams. The brook babbled its way through the night, and all was peaceful.

They were in their favorite sleeping spot, a meadow a few hills over from the cottage, further from the thick pines in an open area where Pa could see in every direction.

The deepest part of night passed as Pa slept. The larger slow moon rose low to the south, bringing some relief to Davy's straining eyes. When it reached the height of the western high peak, brightening the night a little, he would wake Pa.

The half-full slow moon ascended. If Davy watched it, the change in its position was undetectable. If he looked away, scanning the shadows for threats or smiling at the twitching dogs, then looked back, he could tell it had moved.

The night was heaviest at this time, just a bell or two from dawn. Not that they had bells out here like they had in town, but Davy could sense it without the accompanying sound. This was the point when the Five-Faced God I'ya seemed the most distant from their world, when darkness shrouded their world and seemed most threatening. This was the hour when new babies passed through the Gates for unexplained reasons, when curses flew most easily from their malevolent sources and entered the ears of their victims. Even with the slow moon's added light, Davy felt a sense of dread that always accompanied the dark before dawn.

Davy shivered. He should probably wake Pa.

A rustling of grass made him swing his head up the valley. He gripped the crook. His hands sweated.

All was still.

The evening mountain breeze had died out long before, and the morning breeze wouldn't begin until the sun peeked over the eastern ridge.

There it was again, the slightest of sounds, sub-tle enough to be ignored if not for Davy's sharply attuned ears. He clutched the crook til his knuckles whitened, and he gulped dry air. He slowly reached down and tapped Pa's shoulder without looking away from the rustling sound.

Pa grunted and turned his face up, bleary-eyed. He yawned. "Is it time to switch, son?" He bit back the last word as he noticed Davy's expression, but it was too late.

A dog growled, and then a ewe bleated in panic from the edge of the flock, far enough they didn't have a good view of her or the dog. A streak of grey fur flashed by and pounced on a second sheep, rolling the animal as it struggled to get to its feet. White wool darkened with blackish-red spatters as the grey-streaked wolf ripped the sheep's throat out with a violent shake. The dog resting by Davy's feet snarled and flashed after the grey ghastwolf.

The rest of the flock scattered as the wolf pack ambushed from every direction.

Pa yanked at the crook with a yell, and Davy realized he was hanging onto it with both hands. Davy let it go with an effort.

"Behind me, son!" Pa placed himself between Davy and the nearest ghastwolf, a smaller-bodied juvenile without a full mane. Its gray bars were brighter, contrasting with a pure white belly, and its eyes burned yellow in the pale moonlight. Pa swung and bashed it on the nose with his crook. With a yelp, it released the haunch of the sheep under its claws, and it ran.

The dogs' barking and snarling intermixed with that of the wolves. In every direction, Davy heard the sounds of frightened and injured sheep, paws pounding the ground, and the snapping of vicious jaws. He heard one of the dogs yelp in pain.

Then a black silhouette blocked out the stars above and landed nearby. The ground shook.

Even in the night, Davy could see the deep crimson color of the Earth Dragon's wings and scales. Its eyes flashed a bright, almost luminescent red, the way Davy imagined a ruby might be. The pale light of the slow moon seemed to accumulate in those glowing eyes and gleam from its entire body. The dragon whipped its man-sized head across the flock, knocking animals aside. Wolves yelped and sheep screamed in panic as the dragon bared its white fangs the size of Pa's belt knife.

Davy whimpered in fear.

A deep growl behind him caused him to turn, and he met more yellow eyes. The ghastwolf padded closer and crouched. Like the others, it was a juvenile.

Davy stumbled backward with a cry, his knobby knees crumpling beneath him. He landed against Pa, who turned immediately. The whites of his eyes were visible in the night as he raised his crook in a swing.

Pa wasn't quick enough, and the wolf launched itself onto him, knocking Pa down. His head cracked loudly against the rock. Davy curled into a tight ball and clutched Pa's feet as he watched the wolf rip a gash in Pa's neck. Then it moved to Pa's belly and feasted.

The ghastwolf was so close, Davy could have reached out and wiped the blood from its jaw. He could have hit it with Pa's crook, but the crook lay beside Pa, still clenched in one motionless hand.

Davy watched, immobilized with fear and horror. Tears blurred his vision, and the chaos around him became an abstract sea of blood and shadow and red scales and white fur. He heard himself screaming Pa's name. He felt himself shaking Pa's foot. He felt the hard ground beneath him, the flecks of blood and matter hitting his face whenever the wolf shook its head.

He heard more wolves snarling and barking, then yelping, and he wondered whether the dogs were still fighting, or whether they had been ripped apart.

The ghastwolf who killed Pa was suddenly gone. Davy heard a thump as it was knocked off Pa's body, but he couldn't see much beyond a blur of red. More vicious growls paired with a low rumble that Davy felt in his chest.

He crawled up to Pa's face, his legs and arms shaking violently. He squeezed his eyes tightly shut, trying to blink out the tears that flowed like a stream in springtime, but no amount of blinking could get rid of them all. He sniffled and wiped his eyes with his cloak.

Pa lay with his head against the same rock he had slept on. His eyes were closed as if contentedly napping. Below his relaxed expression, his neck was a wreck of torn skin and blood.

Davy couldn't bear to look further down, where Pa's belly had been opened. He put a hand on Pa's cheek, unbelieving.

"Pa?"

He shuddered.

"Pa?"

He couldn't move. He no longer controlled his body, seeing everything from above as though he were an onlooker. Look at that poor boy, he thought, seeing his own gawky self kneeling next to his father's corpse. Look at that poor boy and his poor father.

The flock was scattered, with numerous sheep bleating where they lay, covered in blood. Davy wondered if they would have been less susceptible to injury had they not been sheared less than a week before. Instead of flesh and bone, the ghastwolves would have snapped at thick layers of wool.

He shook his head. It wouldn't have mattered. Ghastwolves were large, and Earth Dragons were even larger. They would tear through any amount of wool to reach the sustenance inside. They would shatter bone with powerful crushing jaws. They would—

His gaze fell back upon Pa's remains. Horrifying reality grounded him, tearing him from his aloof observations and slamming him back to the blood-stained grass, the entrails touching his quivering fingers, and the stillness of Pa's calm sleep.

"Pa?"

Davy knew he should take up Pa's crook and ensure the wolves and dragon had gone. That he should collect the strays before they wandered too far. That he should render aid to the wounded livestock before they bled out.

But he didn't. He couldn't.

All he could do was kneel over Pa and cry.

Ma found him that way as the sun rose. Its bright rays first touched the west face, where Davy could see several Earth Dragons stretching their red wings in the far distance. He stared at their silhouettes with dull eyes.

The sunlight crept downward from stone to sparse trees, kissing the valley with warmth and bringing a new day. Davy would have returned to the cottage to break his fast, then bring a meal to Pa by that hour. Ma must have wondered where he was and left the cottage to make sure he was alright.

He heard her screams before her feet splashing across the stream, and suddenly she appeared next to him, reaching for Pa's head and shouting his name. She cradled him, wept over him, and begged the Eye of I'ya for mercy, for a change of fate. When the sun continued to rise with no answer, she cursed it instead and continued to wail. Then, with a wild look, she dug in her dress pocket and pulled out the wayfarer's blessing, a glass vial filled with a slightly pinkish liquid. She pulled the stopper and sprinkled it over Pa's body, whimpering a prayer to any god that would listen as she did so.

Nothing happened, and she flung the vial as far as she could into the grass.

Davy watched it all, still detached and yet so immersed in his emotions that he couldn't do anything.

He might have stayed that way had Ma not finally shaken him.

"What happened, Davy?" The whites of her eyes had turned pink, and her cheeks were splotchy. Her desperate grip left bloody prints on both his shoulders.

It was a nightmare. Maybe he was feverish and would wake up with Ma patting a cloth on his forehead, a tender smile on her lips.

She shook him again. "Please, Davy..."

"Wolves, Ma," he heard himself say. "Wolves and an Earth Dragon. Pa was sleeping, and I was on watch."

Ma searched his face. Then something in her expression changed, and she released him. She returned to Pa, laying her cheek against his chest and ignoring the filth that adhered to her hair. She wrapped her arms around the corpse, her face turned away from Davy.

"Dig a grave, Davy," she murmured. "The shovel is in the cottage in the corner."

When she said no more, Davy stood to obey. He surveyed the carnage around him. Half the flock was dead or injured. One of the dogs was mauled to pieces and lay with its head in the stream, its tongue lolling. The other limped about, whining and licking at each sheep it encountered. Even in its state, it was trying to gather the herd. Tufts of wool and bits of fur were everywhere, stuck on wisps of grass and slowly bouncing their way upvalley with the gentle morning breeze.

Beyond the terrible scene, surviving sheep moved in tight clusters, looking unsure of where they should go. Some of them limped too.

Davy faltered. Should he round up the sheep first? If they moved downvalley, closer to the ol'Camp-en's flock, they might be safer. Or maybe he should check injuries? He didn't know much beyond binding gashes or light sprains, but Ma knew more and could help. He resolved to carrying medical supplies along with the shovel.

Ma refused to help at first, clutching onto Pa with white knuckles. Her tears had left a damp spot on his chest. However, she got up as Davy finished digging a shallow trench and helped him drag Pa's body into it. She sobbed as she folded his arms across his chest and arranged his head just so.

Davy heaved a sigh as he stared at Pa one last time. Digging had taken him hours already, and his hands ached. Blisters had already formed and burst on his tender hands.

"Cover him, Davy," said Ma. She sniffed loudly.

"I will, Mama, but I'm tired."

"How can you be tired, when you slept during your watch?" she snapped.

He looked up. She glared at him, her chin wrinkled and her lip pouting out in a stiff expression of self-pitying hurt and anger. Her eyebrows knitted, and her tear-filled eyes were directed at him.

Shame flushed through him. "I didn't sleep, Ma," he began.

She collapsed into tears again, mumbling as if to herself. "I should have used the blessing right away. I knew we had bad luck hovering over us." Then she crawled to the nearest sheep and cleaned its wounds.

Davy's heart raced. If he had woken Pa a minute sooner, if he had given Pa the crook more quickly, if he had been more vigilant, this wouldn't have happened. Or maybe, the wolves and dragon had come because of Davy's careless outbursts. Breathing heavily, he forced himself to stand again and shovel dirt over Pa's body. He couldn't look anymore. He didn't want to look.

His raw hands couldn't tolerate more shoveling, and he resorted to scooping the dirt on his hands and knees, shoving it like a dog into the grave. He sobbed as he did so, but tried to avoid wiping his wet face with dirt-encrusted fingers. He ended up doing it anyway, and he knew his cheeks and nose were pasted with muddy streaks.

Pa was gone.

Buried under a layer of dirt in their mountain meadow, Pa was gone, along with his laughter, his kindness, and his patience.

Davy lay back to catch his breath. The sky above was cloudless and empty, no fluffy sheep or pursuing dragons, no pirate ships or myrmaids. The sun had crossed to the other side of the mountains and hung above the peaks. They had lost a day, and still the flock was scattered.

He felt himself scooped in Ma's embrace.

"I'm sorry, Davy," she whispered. She rocked him back and forth for a while, then released him. "Let me help, and then we must get the flock downvalley near the neighbors."

Davy and Ma piled rocks on top of Pa's grave in silence. Davy couldn't help but think of the family they had heard about in town. They had lost their flock, but they hadn't lost a family member. Could he and Ma survive without Pa? Would the wolves or dragons return?

He straightened. Pa would have endured. Pa would have figured out how to survive and thrive. He had loved their beautiful valley, and Davy loved it too. The wolves would not win.

3

Davy worked day and night to be like Pa.

Crook in hand, he watched the flock, guiding them to good grazing during the day and back downvalley at night. He found a somewhat protected low spot by one of the small lakes, partially blocked by a steep bank and by water, enabling him to focus on just one direction at night. He ate and slept with the flock like Pa had so often done, returning to the cottage only when necessary.

The surviving dog limped about like the sheep it herded, but it slept more deeply than it used to, exhausted in its own right from the stress of watching the flock. The sheep that had survived the attack had relatively minor injuries. Ghastwolves tended to target vital organs and violently rip (Davy shuddered at the memory), meaning they either succeeded in killing or failed entirely in their pursuit of quarry.

Davy tended both the dog's and sheep's injuries each day, hoping maybe his thorough care would make up for his failure before.

Ma didn't call on him often. She brought him meals each evening, but she didn't talk much anymore and tended to spend her time in the cottage or alone by Pa's grave. Davy didn't know what to do to console her, for he struggled with it himself. Today, he wove a string of flowers together for her, one to match the wreath he had made for Pa.

He picked at the narrow stems with the tip of his dagger (Pa's dagger), splitting each just enough to slip another stem through it. He produced a long chain of interwoven orange and violet and pink. Ma would like it. Pink and orange together were lucky, as well as pretty.

A sheep bleated from nearby, and Davy jumped to his feet armed with the crook. He scrambled up the bank and looked in every direction, but it was only an elk cow and her baby, sidling their way along the valley edge. The big animal leered suspiciously at him, then ushered her calf further away.

Davy's heartbeat raced for minutes as he watched them disappear into the shadows of evergreens, and he sat down in a different spot where he would have seen them coming. The Eye was high in the sky, a time when ghastwolves slept and dragons lounged on the peaks. Neither hunted this time of day. Nevertheless, Davy was vigilant. He had to be. He spat to one side to defray any bad luck.

The flock had been reduced by a third. That meant a third less wool, a third less milk and cheese, a third less mutton from culls. It also meant a third less coin from Ms. ol'Lannery for essentials they couldn't produce on their own. Davy knew they only needed enough for two, but Pa had done a disproportionate amount of the hard labor.

Somehow Davy and Ma would have to butcher the culls before winter, and next spring shear them all again. Would Ma be able to hang the culls? He looked down at his embarrassingly scrawny arms and heaved a sad sigh. Ma would also have to ride into town on her own for market every few weeks, so Davy could guard the flock. She had already done so a few times, riding the horse and filling the saddlebags instead of taking the cart. This wasn't too unusual, as she had no wool to transport, but Davy wondered again how they would handle things in the spring.

He ushered the flock closer to home near evening, and Ma came out to visit.

Her trudging steps and slumped shoulders contrasted with the smile she pasted on for him, but he could see the tired lines in the corners of her eyes. He offered the string of flowers, and she knelt down so he could lay it around her neck.

"Oh, Davy," she murmured, pulling him into a long hug.

He buried his face in her safe, familiar hold. She smelled like grain flour and butter from her work at home. In that brief moment, he could forget that Pa was missing from their happy, simple life.

"Fall is coming," Ma said in a low, slow voice, one that conveyed what needed to be said without enthusiasm or joy. She had spoken like that since Pa died, as though she were only going through the motions because they were so familiar. Fall harvest in the vegetable garden and then nut and berry foraging. Culling and butchering before winter hit. Spring shearing. And the daily churning of butter from the mothers who still gave milk.

Each season had its own tasks and its own rhythm. Even Davy knew them, despite his shorter years, and he had been mentally preparing for doing them without Pa.

Ma surveyed the flock with glassy eyes. "The older ewes I would have chosen for culling are all gone," she said, seemingly to no one for she didn't look at Davy. Her shoulders slumped even lower. "We've barely enough sheep to make a profit next spring."

"We still have a big flock," Davy said. "Bigger than the ol' Campen's and Ms. ol' Lannery's." He had never thought about it before, but it was true. They even had a horse, something the ol' Campen's didn't have.

"We have to pay tribute to the baron as well, before winter." Ma blinked slowly.

Davy squeezed her hand. The flowers hadn't made anything better. "We don't need much, Ma."

Her breath hitched, and she turned back to him with a tight smile. "We were saving, your father and I. We were saving for an apprenticeship in the Herdsman's Guild."

Davy's eyes widened. "For me?"

She nodded slowly and bit her lip. "What a Herdsmaster you would have made, with a mind just like your father, but I can't afford it now. Not with the losses we took. We'll be lucky to have enough meat through the winter."

"We could sell some of the flock to Ms. ol'Lannery," Davy suggested.

Ma smiled that sad smile. "We may, but that puts us in an even worse state in the spring, with nothing to shear and no wool to sell."

She heaved a long sigh and went back to staring at the sheep, who grazed in contentment, oblivious to their fate as either culls or dragon fodder. Then she slid her gaze up to the mountain peaks, where several Earth Dragons stretched their wings, and a bitter tension grew around her twitching lips.

She stood and turned, but her flower necklace broke and fell away.

Davy opened his mouth to say something, but she had already strode down the hillside in a hurry toward the cottage. Davy stared after her, the broken flower chain hanging from his open palm.

He wasn't Pa.

He couldn't make her laugh, or tell her with assurance that all would be well, or invent a brilliant plan for how they would survive against the odds of a diminished flock with predators on all sides. Pa would have.

He reassessed the valley, looking for threats, then worked to usher the flock closer into the protected area for evening. They bleated at him as they ambled in the general direction. This had been much easier with both dogs, but based on Ma's conversation, they wouldn't get another dog anytime soon either unless a neighbor had puppies they didn't know about.

Davy watched the flock settle safely by the lake, tucked under the steep bank in the safest place he knew. With satisfaction, he settled at a vantage point where he could watch the approach, and he opened the basket of food from Ma. A loaf of bread, a slab of butter, an apple, and pile of fresh-picked kiltberries. He sniffed them appreciatively. The late summer was best for kiltberries, but he hadn't thought Ma had gone foraging lately. If she gathered more, she might make jam for the winter, and that was always something he looked forward to.

He forced himself to only eat the fresh berries and a chunk of bread, for the meal would need to last until Ma visited him again the next night. He swallowed quickly as the Eye of I'ya, the watchful shining orb that moved across the sky each day, dipped under the mountain range to the west. He wanted to be ready, in case anything came for the flock again. He had to be ready, for Ma.

The longest summer days passed, with the only eventful moments being when the antlered herd-beasts passed by in large groups, making their way deeper in the Sikrat to graze on the tender late shoots and blossoms.

Davy relaxed in their presence, knowing their bulls and cows were also watchful and would bugle if they detected something strange. None did. The dragons stayed high on the peaks, and the ghast-wolves stayed away, moving deeper into the moun-tains like they normally did during summer.

Davy thought maybe his luck had changed for the better. Maybe his slips that preceded Pa's death had been forgiven by the fates, and he and Ma could live more peacefully as they tried to prepare for fall.

Ma came to him unexpectedly as the morning sun cast a pinkish hue across the east face. A wide smile stretched across her face, and her shoulders were thrown back. Her pretty waves of freshly-brushed hair tickled her face and blew behind her like a dark halo.

"Bright morning, Davy," she greeted him. It was the first joyful greeting she had given him in months. "Would you like to go to town?"

Davy grinned. The slow moon had cycled more than once since the sweetness of syrup or crumble of pastry had touched his lips. He planted the crook on the ground and pushed himself up, much like Pa would have done. "Is a neighbor coming to watch the sheep?"

Ma shook her head and held out a hand. "I will. You'll go to town on your own. I need you to visit the miller, the blacksmith, and the Herbsman. Can you do that?"

"Can I stop at the bakery?"

She smiled again, her cheeks squeezing up to her eyes and her dimples forming at the corners of her lips. The expression seemed oddly out of place on Ma, making Davy uneasy for a moment, but then he realized it had been months since she had really smiled at him. She continued. "I have an extra quarter-penny just for you, for working so hard. I already took the amount you need from the bottom drawer, and the coin purse is on the table."

Davy whooped with excitement and ran toward the cottage with her hurried instructions in his head. It was a long way, and he eventually slowed to a skip. Ma was putting a lot of trust in him and had given him a whole handful of pennies. The horse needed new shoes before winter, and the shovel handle had broken, and Ma needed a bag of flour. And she wanted another blessing from the Herbsman. And she entrusted all of these tasks to *him*.

He clambered onto the horse, which waited patiently with its saddlebags already seated. He trotted to town with his skinny shoulders thrown back, his shaggy hair blowing back in the breeze, and an unstoppable proud smile cracked across his cheeks.

He stopped first at the smithy, since he thought shoeing might take the longest.

The burly man paused his morning errands, tool sharpening mostly, and glanced up at Davy with light dancing in his eyes. "Well now, what have we here?" he said in a voice made gruff with time. "A new customer? Mr. ol'Sheffed."

Davy swelled with pride. That was what they used to call Pa.

He dug in his little purse and pulled out the number of coins Ma had told him. With his chin held high, he declared, "I'd like some fresh shoes on this horse, please."

The smith chuckled. "Yes, sir. I can do that right quick." He handed a half-penny back to Davy. "And keep that for yourself, son. You and your ma have had a hard season. Get something from the bakery."

Davy's eyes widened with the gift, and he greedily took the half-penny back. He could get another candy with that!

At first, he skipped to the bakery, following the scent of rich fermented dough, but then he stalled. He should buy something for Ma instead. Did she like candies? He chewed on his lip as he thought. Maybe she would like something else.

He passed the seamstress on his way to the bakery. She waved at him through the open door.

The bakery was busier, with several customers lingering in the shop to inhale the heavy scent of baking bread and dense travel cakes. The baker, a stout man who obviously tested his own product on a regular basis, beckoned Davy in.

"Here for a treat, boy? I've some caramels made. Haven't seen you in a long while, not since your dear father passed."

The other customers murmured encouragement, looking at Davy with pitying eyes.

He didn't like that feeling, although he knew they were trying to be nice. He gulped and clenched the coin purse in his hand. A penny and a quarter could buy him several candies, even one of those heavy pound cakes filled with chunks of fruit and sweet vegetables. He had only heard how good they were, for they were a bit too expensive, and meant for long roads like the wayfarers endured. Ma had never bought one for him.

The order was on the tip of his tongue, but he bit it back. Three quarter pennies could also buy something for Ma. With a stuttering apology, he backed out of the shop and returned to the seamstress.

"Bright morning," she called in a friendly tone. He didn't know her, but he knew what she did. He looked over the table, seeing mostly bolts of rough cloth, cloaks and hoods, and other simple garments.

"You need somethin', sweetling?" the woman said.

Davy stuck his hand out. A half and a quarter penny lay in his palm, holding all the power in the world. "I want something for my Ma, please." He didn't know what.

She examined his offering, then curled his fingers over the coins. "Careful how you show that about. I think I have just the thing..." She rummaged in a drawer, laying out several hair pins.

One caught Davy's eye immediately, a yellow flower sewn in bunches of dyed cloth and affixed to a copper clasp. It reminded him of the round flowers that popped up in the driest rocks, shooting up a single stalk with a large cluster flower knee-high. What did Tara call it? Mountain corn flower? Or was that a different one? After a month, the yellow leaves would give way to puffy white fuzzies that blew away in the wind.

The seamstress nodded approval of his choice. "And best yet, this one doesn't cost quite that much." She pressed the quarter-penny back into his hand. "I know you were headed to the bakery before."

Elated, Davy tucked the pretty hairpin into his pocket and ran back to the bakery for a caramel.

He returned to the smithy and sucked happily on his candy until the man had finished with the horse. As Davy made to mount, the smithy put a staying hand on his shoulder.

"Are you planning to butcher any of the flock this fall?"

Davy wasn't really sure.

"If you do, call upon us for help," the smith answered with an encouraging look. Not a smile, but an odd stiffening of the lips as though he were resolute to help, but recognized how tragic it was that he needed to offer. "The butcher and I are both willing to come up for a day to help your ma. You let her know, alright?"

Davy nodded and thanked the big man.

The smith dusted red powder on the horse's feet once again. "A village helps its own, boy. Your father was a good man and a loyal customer. It's the least we can do. Now get you home."

Davy stopped at the miller on his way out of town, filling the saddlebags with sacks of flour. Each trip garnered some supplies for immediate use, but more for the coming winter. Ma would store most of the flour away for the harder times that were coming soon.

As Davy cantered out of town, again raising his chin as he passed the tavern and hoping the tavern-keeper would also see how independent and capable he was, he pondered the impending winter. Having the smith and butcher help with culls could save them, if they had anything to cull. Ma still didn't seem sure she could afford to diminish the flock any further. They would lack for meat, dried and smoked, but they would be able to survive on vegetables and bread. The bigger issue, she said, was that the sale of some of the mutton would have paid for more grain for the sheep to bolster their diet during the worst snows.

He reached the cottage, which was quiet as he had expected. Ma was no doubt with the flock further up the valley, waiting for him to relieve her.

He unloaded the saddlebags, awkwardly lowering them to the ground from up high, then struggled to unsaddle the horse and brush her down. He wasn't quite tall enough for all these chores yet, and he was exhausted by the time he was done. He patted the horse's nose.

"Good girl," he murmured affectionately. "I hope you like your new shoes."

She whickered at him and went to graze.

Davy finished putting everything away, then patted his pocket to ensure the hairpin was where it belonged. He walked slowly, enjoying the beautiful afternoon as he made his way toward Ma. As he crested a hill, he smiled. Tiny specks of white told him his instincts were right.

Ma had ushered the flock up to the open meadow near Pa's grave, a good spot for the daytime with all the clover and the babbling brook. And of course, she could be near Pa. Davy often did the same thing, refreshing Pa's grave with grassy wreaths and fresh-picked flowers every week.

As Davy got closer, he could see Ma's figure. She faced away from him, and she leaned against the pile of rocks erected for Pa. She held the crook at an odd angle, as though she were asleep.

Davy thought that wasn't surprising. This was a fairly safe time of day to nap, as the predators didn't seem to like coming out under the heat and stern glare of the Eye. Afternoons were peaceful.

He called to her when he got closer, but she couldn't hear him.

He quickened his step, grinning as he pulled the hairpin from his pocket.

He called again, but she didn't move.

"Ma, I'm back," he cried, breathless as he came around to face her where she napped.

Ma lay with her head against the cairn, her shoulders sagged in restful slumber. A small relieved smile was on her lips.

"Ma?"

Davy dropped to his knees, banging one on a jutting rock.

Ma's delicate white skin was marred on both forearms by long red lines. Her knuckles lay in pools of blood that seeped into the ground and stained the cream fabric of her dress. A paring knife lay loosely in one hand, the crook hung in the other. She didn't move.

Davy stared at her for a long time, trying to understand.

She had seemed happy when he left, happier than he had seen her in a long time. She had given him tasks that implied her trust, that indicated he was old enough to take on some of the chores as they prepared for winter. And he thought he had done a good job.

He chewed on his bottom lip, drawing blood.

Was he not worth living for?

Shame knocked him over like an avalanche tumbling down the mountainside. Shame for thinking such a terrible thing about Ma. Shame for not helping enough. Shame for living when Pa had died and for being bad luck. He fell into Ma's cold, stiff frame as he sought the familiar essence of comfort. It was gone.

Nonetheless, he curled up next to her and cried for a while, wishing somehow she and Pa would come back.

Now he understood why Ma had wanted him to fix the shovel. He had another hole to dig. He couldn't bear to do it tonight, but if he didn't something might drag her off.

Resigned, he stumbled back to the cottage to retrieve the shovel and a night's worth of food.

If he thought while he dug, maybe he would think of a plan. A plan to survive. He barely knew how to bake bread, and he couldn't do all the things Ma did while also guarding the flock. He had no idea what to do.

He placed Ma next to Pa, like she would have wanted. His labors took him into the evening, and darkness fell over the valley.

Normally, he would have moved the flock somewhere else, as this meadow was the one where he had lost Pa, but ...he didn't know what else to do. The sheep naturally clustered in close and slept soundly, dim white patches visible in the moonlight.

Davy packed the earth as best he could over Ma's body, then made another pile of rocks over her to match Pa's. With a heavy sigh, he placed the yellow hairpin on top.

He blinked at it, still confused, utterly lost as to what to do next.

Despite all he had done, trying to help, he had not been enough to fill Pa's boots. He was too young, too weak, too worthless to do all the things that needed done. And Ma must have realized it. There was no way to get through the winter without Pa. Even if they did, with the smith and butcher's help, then what? They would have to survive the following spring's work, and the fall after that, and the winter after that.

Ma must have seen the hopelessness in it all.

Davy sat on the very rock upon which Pa had sat. Maybe Pa would bless him with an idea from the other side of the Gates. Maybe, now that he and Ma were together, they could think of something smart to help Davy survive.

Or maybe Davy was alone.

Completely and entirely alone.

4

THE NEXT MORNING BROUGHT no relief. A flurry of confused thoughts warred with each other in his mind. Should he ride to town and ask for help, leaving the flock alone? Should he grit his teeth and stay, surviving *somehow*? Chewing the last of his crusty bread (Ma had made it), he dabbed at the crumbs on his lap and then took a long draught from the babbling stream. He knew, deep inside where a chasm had opened, where his heart had been, he couldn't stay where he was.

He took one more long look at the pair of graves, one with fine threads of grass pushing through and one so fresh the insects were still crawling through the sod.

He needed help, and surely those who had seen him working so hard would see that he had no other alternative. That's how it worked.

So he saddled the horse, packed a few supplies, and ushered the flock downvalley with the help of the limping dog. They worked their way one hill and hummock at a time, over rocks and mini-waterfalls, down to the next valley where their closest neighbors, the ol'Campens, lived.

The flock resisted, wanting only to graze in the warm morning sun and nurse their bruises and cuts, and Davy continually had to urge them onward. He finally reached his destination as the Eye reached its zenith, seeing Mr. ol'Campen from afar.

The man raised an arm in greeting, then beckoned Davy closer. "What's this, boy? Why've you got the flock so far from home?" Mr. ol'Campen drew his brows together and squinted up the valley. "Where's your mother?"

Davy gulped, unable to say aloud why. He felt his lips moving, but no sound came out, and he eventually closed his mouth.

"Boy?" Mr. ol'Campen caught the horse's reins and looked up at Davy.

Davy began to shake, and he slumped in the saddle, suddenly feeling the weight of everything he had been bearing. He stuttered, but again no words came out.

Mr. ol'Campen scanned the sad-looking flock and the limping dog, then patted Davy's knee. "I'll watch the sheep for you, boy. Go on to the missus and tell her what you need."

Davy rode alone to the cottage, a quaint log home set upon a small hill, surrounded by a large fenced garden. He dismounted awkwardly from the big animal and tied her reins around the fence post.

Mrs. ol'Campen, a spindly middle-aged woman with an over-gaunt face but a generous smile, stood from her weeding and wiped sweat from her brow with a dirty hand. "Why, Davy, what're you doin' here this time o'day? Come in, come in. Did your mother send you for somethin'?"

Davy fumbled with the gate, locking it in place behind him as he continued to search for words. Instead, he found himself reaching for Mrs. ol'Campen, his vision blurring as the tears flooded out. He buried himself in her warm embrace. Her arms were scrawnier than Ma's, and her chest less buxom, but her affectionate hold was nevertheless comforting as she tucked her chin over his hair and hugged him back.

Mothers knew how to hug, and when. She held him tightly until he took a sniffling breath.

"What's this, Davy? What's wrong?"

He stuttered the words out with an effort. "Ma's gone."

Mrs. ol'Campen's consternation was conveyed through a sudden stiffening of her hold, and she turned his face up to hers. Her cheeks were tight, and her dark eyes wide. "She left you?"

He shook his head slightly. "She's with Pa."

Mrs. ol'Campen's lips parted in shock, and then fear passed over her face as she lowered her voice. "Wolves? Dragons? What happened, Davy?" She pushed him back to scan him over, swiveling him from side to side with a mother's eye. "Are you alright? Did they hurt you?"

"No." His quiet admission made her pause. "No, she left on her own."

Mrs. ol'Campen's eyebrows raised with pity and horror, and she pursed her lips.

"I brought the flock," he continued, launching into a litany of his hard work. "I brought the horse and some grain and some money, and I buried Ma and put the shovel away, and closed up the flour before I left, and I...I made the house nice like Ma would like it. And I kept them all safe down to Mr. ol'Campen, and I was hoping that you might watch them with yours for a day while I ride into town and see if maybe Ms. ol'Lannery will buy them. And I can pay you for your trouble." He was rambling as he stuck his hands into his purse, which he had stuffed with all the coin he could find, and he displayed a handful for Mrs. ol'Campen.

He stammered. "I'm sorry if it's a burden. I can work for you too, if that's not enough."

Mrs. ol'Campen shook his shoulders and stared at him. "Davy, stop. Yer not goin' to town to sell your sheep to that stingy woman, yer not goin' anywhere." She ushered him to a wooden log that served as a bench next to the house. "Put your money away, boy. Your ma really is..." Her voice rang high in question, but she answered herself. "By the Light, I wouldn't have thought—"

She clucked with disapproval and shook her head. "Not that it changes a thing. Yer here now. Y'did well bringing the flock down. Mr. ol'Campen can easily watch them with Mikkel's help. He ought to return from gathering nuts soon with Tara. You'll just stay with us til we figure a way through, Davy. Okay?" She squeezed his shoulders again and waited for a response.

Davy nodded dumbly but didn't look her in the eye. She was being so kind, and yet it made him ache deep inside. As if her warmth and comfort served only to heighten the awfulness of Ma's abandonment, the way a bright summer day under a cloudless sky made the shade seem darker.

"There now, put that money safe away. Good. Now you want to make yerself busy, then help me with this weeding."

"Can you teach me to make bread?"

Mrs. ol'Campen squinted at him. "That I can."

Davy gnawed on his raw lip. If he learned that, maybe he could take care of himself.

Then again, what if he was allowed to stay? A ray of hope shone as he looked at Mrs. ol'Campen, who had returned to her weeding with a low humming. What was one more little boy, when you already had two older children? He wouldn't eat much, and he would work very hard, as hard as he could. If he made himself useful, maybe she and Mr. ol'Campen would let him stay.

On the other hand, he was one more mouth to feed through the coming winter, and he wasn't nearly as useful as Mikkel and Tara. Mikkel was tall and strong, old enough to hunt on his own and lead Tara through the wooded mountainside, big enough to hold the sheep during shearing and fight an attacking ghastwolf. Tara was over a hand taller than Davy and as capable as her mother, able to identify plants and make medicines and cook delicious food.

What could Davy possibly provide that they needed?

He scrambled onto his knees to pull the stubborn roots from between the carrots. Mrs. ol'Campen worked beside him with a bit more grunting as she shifted from a crouch to standing and back, but together they cleared the row.

She clapped her hands half-clean with satisfaction and then patted his head. "Yer a fine boy, Davy. Don't worry now, yer with us. We'll take care of you til we figure things out."

Davy received a bedroll next to Mikkel and a place near the hearth when they ate. He helped weed every day, much like he had in the garden back home, making the ol'Campen's garden an orderly set of lines of green foliage and colorful vegetables and fruits. He pored over bushy plants for the nasty fat worms that chewed on fresh leaves and crawled through the squash vines looking for beetles and their tiny white egg clusters. He carried buckets of water from the stream during the hottest weeks, giving the thirsty plants relief from drought.

But his favorite times were with Tara, who had declared his knowledge of plants to be inadequate for a resident of the lush valleys and evergreen slopes of the Sikrat.

She skipped ahead on a narrow trail, the dirt track pounded to white dust by countless elk does and their babies. Small rodents, dappled in white spots like the sunlight dappled the forest floor, skittered away as they came too near. Tara leapt on top of a fallen log, flinging her arms wide and balancing as she stepped down its length.

Davy grinned and followed.

Tara hunkered down with a gasp. "Look, Davy! A fowlfeather mushroom, good for eating."

Davy wrinkled his nose at the orange-streaked slab protruding from the log. Its curled edges frilled out in hundreds of white tendrils. "It doesn't *look* good for eating," he mumbled.

Tara laughed. "The center part cooks like a steak, and Mama will chop the edges up for stew so you don't notice the funny texture as much." She pulled out her belt knife and carefully cut the slab from the log, allowing the smaller slabs beneath it to continue growing. Then she ran around in a wide circle, tapping it by three other tree bases.

"Why did you do that?" Davy asked.

"Good luck," she replied stoutly as she placed the mushroom in the loose-woven satchel that hung at her hip. "It will make more mushrooms grow, but you gotta do it three times."

They continued on, finding more fowlfeather mushrooms in the damp nooks near streams, then a different, drier kind on the dying pines that still stood.

Davy sat on Tara's shoulders to reach them, which made both of them laugh wildly as he chopped at the flatter shelf mushroom with his own blade. It was hard as a rock in his hands, and he looked doubtfully down at Tara.

"It's for medicine," she giggled, helping him down and taking the dark brown chunk into her sack. "You grind it up and make it into tea for sickness."

"What's it taste like?"

"Like chewing on a piece of wood." She grimaced.

They both giggled, then continued on to a hillside covered in kiltberries. Davy pulled his own canvas sack out, plucking each berry from its delicate hold on the thorned bushes. They both kept a wary eye for odd sounds, knowing the smaller bears liked berries too, but they heard nothing beyond the chatter of birds and the scampering of squirrels and mice. Tara showed him several flowers and another type of berry, this one a crimson cluster that grew on certain flowerheads. It mixed with the brown mushroom, she said, for when you were really sick, and might even save your life.

Davy listened and learned, but more than anything, he had fun. He had enjoyed seeing Tara and Mikkel before and had often wondered what it was like to have a sibling. Maybe this was what it was like.

Davy realized he did know something useful and took the lead caring for his horse. The ol' Campen's didn't have much room for her in the stable, as they had never owned a horse. Their sheep flock was smaller than Davy's, and their belongings somewhat simpler although they did have a cow for milking. Having a horse available was a great boon, something they appreciated and utilized after he offered. Sometimes Mikkel rode her into town, and sometimes Mrs. ol'Campen and Tara rode into town together.

Davy helped them become more comfortable with the horse's behavior, taught them to saddle and mount her, and then to ride with greater ease. When they returned from town, saddlebags full of whatever supplies they had gone to retrieve and emptied of garden vegetables they had sold, they always called upon him. Mikkel and Tara helped reach the high spots as he showed them how to brush her down and check for chafing from the halter. Then check her ears and teeth and feet, then reward her with a handful of grain.

Maybe he could contribute something, he thought, swelling a little with pride.

They continued on, and Davy realized they had decided to let him stay for at least a little while.

Was he their son now?

Guilt gnawed at him as he chewed his lip, breaking it open and tasting blood. Would Ma and Pa be mad? He hadn't visited their graves since burying Ma. He had been too busy helping, trying to prove his worth, and part of him had been too horrified by his reality to look at the twin cairns in the light of day.

Pa's flowers had likely dried up and blown away, and Ma's copper hairpin had probably fallen, half-green with rust as it buried itself in the dirt.

He wouldn't find out.

He entered a familiar rhythm as the weather cooled and the brisk winds ushered a glacial chill from the high mountaintops down into the valley. The days shortened and the nights lengthened, but Davy thought it might be alright because the evenings were spent stirring the stewpot and helping Mrs. ol'Campen with chores. He learned to prepare the edible mushrooms they foraged in the forest, and he churned butter. (Mikkel teased him when he commented on how funny the butter tasted, and he realized he had never eaten cow butter before.) Tara taught him to make kiltberry jam and infused honey, and seemingly a thousand other things from the treasures she found in the mountains, and he found himself constantly in awe of her store of knowledge.

"Your family is really lucky to have you," he said once, marveling at the fragrant rabbit-mushroom stew she tended.

Tara smiled as she stirred the pot and sprinkled something ground into it. "I just like exploring and learning what everything is. Some of it turned out to be useful."

"But you know everything." His wide eyes, which he exaggerated, made her giggle, and he grinned at his own success.

Then she shrugged. "I learn a lot from the Herbsman, I suppose. He sometimes suggests taking me as an apprentice, but I doubt I'll ever be able to do that."

Davy thought of Ma, her resigned half-smile as she suggested Davy could have become a Herdsmaster, if only they had the money. "Why not?"

"It costs too much to enter the Temple and apprentice," said Tara, affirming Davy's suspicions. She sighed. "But it's okay. I like living here and being with my family." She caught herself with a sharp breath and apologized.

Her words had made his stomach sour for a moment, but he really did understand, and he told her so. Before losing Ma and Pa, he had wanted nothing but to live in the valley, tending sheep and enjoying each day under the Eye. Life had been simple, his purpose clear. He had loved the reliable monotony, a rhythm that ebbed and flowed with the seasons. The thought of Callendera, that distant and foreign place where Herdsmen went to train in livestock husbandry, terrified him.

Mrs. ol'Campen entered the cottage bearing freshly picked greens, and Davy rushed to close the door for her. She beamed at him, laying the unruly pile of loose leaves on the table. "Thank ye, Davy. Tara, dear, is the stew ready fer some greens?" She roughly chopped the greens and tossed them in to soften, then clapped her hands together with satisfaction and sat at the table. "That's a nice stew fer these cooler evenin's. Mikkel's rabbit, Tara's mushrooms, 'n' Davy's vegetables."

"My vegetables?" Davy pointed a finger at his own chest in surprise.

Mrs. ol'Campen pulled him on her lap and hugged him. "Y'worked very hard to tend the garden, didn't ye? Y'kept the bugs off and the weeds away, and y'made sure the late-planted lettuce had enough water during the heat so it could thrive now in the cold."

Davy flung his arms around Mrs. ol'Campen and buried his face in her hair, and she held him tight. She didn't smell like Ma, but she hugged like she did.

"I'm very proud of ye, Davy," she said.

A flicker of light sparked inside him, fed by his pride in knowing he had done well, and he clung to Mrs. ol'Campen with all the strength he had. *Davy's vegetables.* He contributed something, like Mikkel and Tara did, and Mrs. ol'Campen noticed. Maybe, if he kept going, kept working, he could stay with them forever.

5

As AUTUMN SET IN, Davy learned the basics of making and kneading dough, then baking it in the heat of the fire. Mrs. ol'Campen had him tend the hearth as well, and he became more comfortable with that task as long as he didn't have to chop the wood. Mikkel usually did that, splitting the cut logs with precision, his lean muscles making each swing as efficient as possible.

Mikkel tried to teach Davy how to use the maul, how to use its own weight to power the swing and not waste energy, but Davy thought it was very difficult. The maul often fell at an odd angle, bouncing off instead of snapping through, and Davy would get frustrated as well as exhausted. He kept trying though, because Mikkel had to do all the other work gathering firewood: felling trees with the axe, sawing logs into chunks, and carrying the pieces to the house. Mikkel's days were consumed with hunting and collecting wood for the winter, while Davy was consumed with guilt over his inability to help more.

Then one day, he had an idea. He had already suggested the horse be used to drag the logs from the woods to the house, but sometimes they were too large or awkward.

Mikkel hefted a cut piece into the pile with a grunt.

"What if we got the horse cart?" Davy suggested.

Mikkel's eyes lit up, and the older boy wiped sweat from his forehead. "That would be great. Back at your house?" Mikkel nodded slowly as he assessed the growing wood pile, still catching his breath. "That would be great," he repeated.

Davy mentioned the idea that evening as the family ate supper. Although Mikkel had gone to relieve his father in the fields, Davy spoke for him, suggesting they use the cart to help move cut logs to the house more quickly.

Mrs. ol'Campen ruffled his hair. "Why Davy, that's so thoughtful, and a fine idea."

Mr. ol'Campen agreed. "Ye know, boy, the missus and I have had a talk, and we've got t'thinking that ye ought to stay here."

Davy's heart fluttered as he set his fork down and stared. "You mean, forever?" His voice seemed small, even to himself.

Mr. and Mrs. ol'Campen exchanged smiles with each other, then looked at him. Mrs. ol'Campen put a warm hand on his cheek and nodded.

Tara's delighted gasp broke the silence, and she grabbed his arm in excitement. "Praise the Light, Davy. That means you'll be my brother!"

Davy could hardly believe it. A wide grin cracked across his face and strained his cheeks, and warm tears welled up from somewhere deep within. It was strange to feel so happy, so relieved. His hard work had paid off. He spent the evening in shock, continually glancing at Mr. ol'Campen for looks of approval, and finally curling up in his bed near the low-burning fire with a sigh of contentment. Mrs. ol'Campen tucked him in and kissed his forehead, just as she did Tara, and he slid into a peaceful sleep.

The next morning, Mrs. ol'Campen sent Mikkel and Tara up the valley to retrieve the horse cart and Davy's other belongings.

"No sense in leavin' useful things if yer stayin' here," said Mrs. ol'Campen with an encouraging hug around his shoulders as the older children left with his horse. "Don't worry now. You didn't want to go with them, did ye?"

Davy shook his head. The thought of raiding the cupboards and drawers, of leaving the mattress barren of its fur, of leaving the cottage as empty as his heart had been was too painful to face. Mikkel and Tara would do it without confronting its ugliness.

"I thought not," murmured Mrs. ol'Campen, holding him close.

They celebrated the heavy-laden wagon's return with shouts of laughter and the dog's howling. His limp had finally disappeared, and he sprinted back and forth between the mixed flock and the oncoming cart.

Tara and Mikkel had brought everything they could. Spare parts for the wagon, extra tools and cutlery, clothes and blankets, items from the horse's stall, and grains Ma had stored away. Mrs. ol'Campen went about tucking the various supplies and tools about their log home. She laid the familiar fur on Davy's cot, tucking his rag knight underneath with its tattered head poking out. Then she sorted through the dried foods and flour, humming a song as she worked.

"The worms had gotten in and eaten some of it, so we left one bag of flour," said Tara, wrinkling her nose in disgust. "But we got most of it cleaned out, and we found a few spare tunics and pants." She pulled them out and held them against Davy's body. They were large.

"Those were Pa's," he mumbled, feeling a sharp pang of sadness.

Tara insisted on holding up another shirt to see, then looked at him. "They're yours now, Davy. You'll grow into them. I can probably size one of them down to fit you."

"You need a bath and a change of clothes anyway," Mikkel chuckled, waving his hand under his nose, but Tara shoved him and rolled her eyes.

"We all do, now that the sowing season is over." Mrs. ol'Campen broke them up with an overly stern scowl. She pulled out the one spare dress (Ma's dress) and held it against herself, and again Davy felt pain cut through his heart. Mrs. ol'Campen then held the dress against Tara, who was shorter than she. "We'll have to take all of these in, but that's alright. What a blessing you've brought to our family, Davy."

When the onions were pulled and dried, hung in stringers from the ceiling, and the potatoes were dug and scrubbed, Mrs. ol'Campen sent Davy to fetch bucket after bucket of fresh water from the brook. She filled the clean stewpot and brought it to a boil, then dumped it into a large tub for baths.

Although he and Mikkel had rinsed off in the numbing cold of the stream many times, this was the first hot bath Davy had since he arrived. He shivered with excitement and thought of the fresh tunic waiting for him, recently resized by Tara's careful hand. Davy's chest was scrawny compared to Pa's, and Tara had teased that she could make two Davy-sized shirts out of the original. He didn't mind. The tunic reminded him of Pa, and he would wear it happily.

When it was finally Davy's turn, the water was tepid but still welcome. Mrs. ol'Campen started with his scruffy hair, working soap into it with sure hands until the bubbles ran down his temple.

He splashed at the bubbles with joy. Ma used to wash his hair too, her strong fingers massaging his temple and running through his hair until it squeaked with cleanliness.

"By the Light, Davy, you were due for a good wash," Mrs. ol'Campen muttered as she rinsed his hair. She started scrubbing his shoulders and neck with a rag. "A good season of labor earned you some honest sweat, and now we'll get you all clean."

He grinned at her as she raised his arms up and scrubbed underneath one side at a time. He thought he could feel the layer of salty grime coming off, even though he rinsed frequently in the stream. There was just something different about a hot, soapy bath, especially when someone motherly scoured your skin pink. To be clean!

"Okay, did you get yer legs? Your feet and between your little toes?" She nodded with satisfaction as he stuck each foot out of the water and wriggled them. "Good boy. Stand up now, and we'll get yer lower back and ye'll be all done."

Davy obeyed, and Mrs. ol'Campen began to scrub the middle of his back, down to his rump, and behind his ribs. An irresistible giggle burst from him as he twitched away from the sensitive spots.

She paused, the rag coming to a stop on his left side.

He glanced back at her, still giggling, but then his breath caught in his throat.

Her thin brows knitted and unknitted as she stared at his back with frightened, rapidly blinking eyes. The cloth dabbed erratically on his skin as her hands began to shake.

Her fear infected him, and a pit formed in the middle of his stomach. He didn't understand what was wrong with her. All of her motherly warmth was suddenly gone, an extinguished lamp that left him plunged in darkness.

She staggered to her feet, the rag limp in one hand, and her mouth worked furiously for moments. Then she shouted outside for Mikkel without looking away. She was staring at Davy as if he were a dangerous predator, a terrifying Earth Dragon or a rabid ghastwolf.

And he began to wonder if there was something wrong with himself.

Mikkel poked his head into the cottage with a confused look at Davy, who still stood in the tub feeling somewhat embarrassed. At least Tara wasn't around. Mikkel slid inside and shut the door, then approached with a questioning look at his mother.

"Look at that," said Mrs. ol'Campen, pointing at Davy's back with a trembling finger.

Mikkel came around slowly, giving Davy an apologetic half-smile. Davy felt his cheeks burning, and he then heard Mikkel's sharp intake of breath.

He touched Davy's back, poking at him and then stretching his skin one way and then the other.

If not for the fear twisting his insides apart, he would have reacted to the ticklish feeling. Instead, he craned his neck to try and see what they were seeing. What was wrong with him?

"The Mark." Mikkel's voice was low and serious, as threatening as the growl of a ghastwolf. He groaned and backed away.

Davy shuddered. What did he mean by that? The Mark of Evil? Davy twisted, trying to see for himself, but it was too high on his ribcage, just in that spot he couldn't see over his shoulder. Ms. ol'Lannery had spoken of the Mark, how it cursed people, how it was removed early in life so other people wouldn't be infected by its influence. Panic welled up inside.

Mrs. ol'Campen agreed. "That's what I thought. To think, they *kept* him." Something in her tone had altered from that soothing singsong she had used before as she scrubbed Davy's hair, as she wiped bubbles onto the round tip of his nose with a laugh. Her expression was stiff, cold, and afraid. And she looked at him with distrustful eyes, as though he had done something terrible.

Mikkel did the same.

"Should I get out?" he ventured, trying not to cry although he felt his chest spasming with the effort. He stepped out of the tub and reached for the drying cloth next to Mikkel.

Mikkel stepped back further as he did so, then backed all the way to the door. "I'll get Papa." He disappeared.

Davy dried himself and dressed awkwardly, feeling the interminable stare of Mrs. ol'Campen. She no longer helped. He had expected her to scruff his hair dry, to pat the damp spots on his back, to help slip his head and arms through the right holes in his clean tunic. Like Ma used to do.

Instead she sat on one of the chairs, watching him with her brow furrowed and her eyes bulging wide. Her gaunt face was turned to a deep frown, which pulled both of her cheeks taut and created a wrinkle where her dimples should have been.

Mr. ol'Campen burst in, panting somewhat from his hurry. Davy cowered under his presence, which felt threatening for the first time ever. Mr. ol'Campen spun him around and yanked up his tunic to examine his back.

"By I'ya," came Mr. ol'Campen's gruff voice. "I wouldn't have believed it. The boy is cursed."

"What do we do?" asked Mrs. ol'Campen. "We've let it into our home." Davy could hear the horror in her wavering question.

Mr. ol'Campen shook his head and turned Davy back around to look at his face. Like his wife, his expression had turned cold and detached, no longer affectionate in any way. "We can't allow it to stay. You've seen what it wrought on the ol'Sheffeds." He shoved Davy away, and he stumbled to his rear on the straw-covered dirt floor.

Davy couldn't hold back his tears anymore. He didn't understand. He knew the Mark was bad, but he couldn't even see it. And what did it mean now? They had already adopted him.

"I thought I could stay," he said between shaky breaths as Tara burst in, a wild look on her face.

She ran toward him, but both Mikkel and her father caught her arms and held her back. "Davy, it'll be alright," she cried. "It doesn't matter."

"It does," her father corrected. "You know it does."

Tara strained, but neither Mikkel nor Mr. ol'Campen would release her. "But he didn't do any-thing."

"His mere existence is a bane upon those around him," said Mr. ol'Campen. "Now we know why such terrible things befell his family. It's only a matter of time before that bad luck affects us." He finally acknowledged Davy. "Sorry, boy, but we can't let you stay."

Davy's insides dropped. "But you said I was part of your family now."

Mr. ol'Campen shook his head and grimaced. "It cannot be. We have to take care of ourselves first."

Davy's sobs were loud in the small room, and he struggled to speak between gasping breaths. "But I can help. I'll work harder."

"That's not enough, boy. Not with a curse of evil hanging over you. We're heading into winter, the hardest season of all, and I don't want to draw any wolves or dragons here." Mr. ol'Campen said the last part softly, as though even mentioning the possibility would bring them near.

Davy stared. Was Mr. ol'Campen implying that he was to blame for Pa dying? For Ma's depression? For everything? The truth of it knocked Davy down like rocks in an avalanche, beat him into the floor where he sat. Mr. ol'Campen was surely right. Davy was cursed, or rather a curse in himself. A living curse of death and bad things.

"Should we give him to the next Gate?" Mrs. ol'Campen's suggestion was met with pondering silence as the family looked at each other.

Tara shouted a protest and yanked against her father and brother's firm grips, but they all ignored her.

Mrs. ol'Campen would no longer look at Davy, instead continuing as if Tara hadn't said anything. "It's only right. They should have dealt with it as soon as the midwife inspected him."

Mr. ol'Campen nodded agreement. Mikkel looked apologetic, but didn't speak up, for there was also a gleam of fear in his eyes.

The pit in Davy's stomach gurgled into a bundle of sickening terror, and he felt faint. He heard himself begging them to let him stay, and he heard Tara shouting that they had claimed him as their son. That he was her brother now. Until Mr. ol'Campen struck her in the face and told her to gather his things. She began to cry too but obeyed, wordlessly shuffling past Davy to help Mrs. ol'Campen.

Mikkel pulled Davy up from the floor and ushered him outside, and at first Davy thought the older boy was being kind. Then he realized he was being pushed, shoved out the door and through the garden gate.

"Wait here," mumbled Mikkel, turning back to the house. A few minutes later, Mikkel came back out with Davy's saddle and bags, and he helped him ready his horse. He filled the bags with flour and a few other supplies, then helped Davy mount.

"Where's Tara?" Davy asked.

Mikkel shook his head and didn't answer.

Instead, he and Mr. ol'Campen walked Davy to the flock, and Mr. ol'Campen picked up the fallen crook which Tara had abandoned earlier. Pa's crook. Mr. ol'Campen held it as though it were a snake and handed it up to Davy. "You may take your sheep and dog, boy, but yer on your own. Ye'll have to take 'em back upvalley."

Mikkel handed the reins up to Davy, and the ol'Campen men ushered their flock apart, the work eased by the presence of two people and their own dogs. They moved away, never looking back at him again.

A family.

Davy sat still on his horse long enough that she bored. She stretched her neck down toward the grassy meadow, pulling the reins from his loose fingers, and they slipped from his grip to hang freely.

He fumbled for them, breaking through the dark whirlwind of confusion in his mind, but they had fallen too far to reach. He gripped at the horse's mane, working himself up her neck with his legs pushed back against the stirrups. He reached her flickering ears and yanked on the halter, finally catching the reins with the tips of his fingers. He flipped the loop around her head so he wouldn't drop them again, then looked back up.

The ol' Campens were gone.

Heaving a long sigh that barely expressed his resignation or heartbreak, he gathered his sheep and pushed them upvalley.

Toward the empty cottage. Toward Ma and Pa. Toward home.

6

THE VEGETABLE GARDEN WAS overgrown, dense with unkempt weeds and overripe, beetle-infested squash.

Davy regretted his choice to abandon the cottage to the ol' Campen's decisions. They had taken almost everything of use and returned only what fit in his saddlebags, such a rush were they in to get him away from their family.

He had his coin purse, a tightly rolled fur, a few pounds of dried meat and berries, and some grain, but that was all. The cottage contained a few spare tools, a butter churner and a spade. As Tara had mentioned, a bag of worm-infested flour lay in the corner, muddled with webbing but mostly full. He found the paring knife with which Ma had ended her life tucked in the back of a drawer.

Davy slumped in the middle of the forgotten garden, his rear sensing the damp soil through his thin pants. He mindlessly tugged at weeds and chewed on his lip as he pondered what to do. The dog, who had faithfully followed, licked his cheek once before returning to the flock nearby.

It had taken half a day to get the sheep home, and he would have to pass by the ol' Campens again to get to town. They had told him not to come near now that they knew he was cursed, but maybe he could slip by if they were in a distant field.

If Ms. ol' Lannery was interested in buying his animals, he had to at least try to usher them to town. He wasn't confident he could handle them through the winter, and he knew he couldn't cull any alone. No meat, no meat sales, no jerky for winter beyond that which the ol' Campens had given him.

He looked up to the peaks, spying the familiar orange-red of Earth Dragons who oversaw the valley. And in that moment, he considered giving up.

If he got on the horse and rode away, he might find a place he belonged, where no one knew he bore the Mark. He jiggled the coin purse on his belt. Maybe he could ride to Callendera and join the guild like Ma and Pa had wanted. Did he have enough?

No, Ma said he didn't.

However, maybe he would if he sold the entire flock.

Davy, the ol'Sheffed without any sheep, the one who lost the flock that had been developed over generations. He shook his head. He couldn't betray all of Pa's years of hard work by selling now.

Then it struck him how absurd his weeding was. The vegetables were all overdone, onions flopped over and carrots growing woody in the centers.

In a fury, he began yanking everything out. He smeared his cheeks into mud as he worked through his tears. Dirt shoved itself beneath his formerly clean-scrubbed nails, forming black crescents.

As the sun sank low, he dragged a pile of unwashed vegetables into the cottage.

There was no time to drive the sheep further from the timber that crowded the cottage. They would have to sleep here for the night. He re-emerged with a carrot and his crook, placing himself in the center of the flock. The dog circled, pushing the sheep into a tighter circle around him, and Davy tried to stay awake.

He failed, nodding off sometime after the sun went down and the quick moon had already moved partway across the sky.

A bleating cry was the only warning he had that something was wrong, and the large shadow of a lone ghastwolf flashed away with white in its jaws. The dog snarled at its heels, nipping until Davy heard a yelp, and the scuffle ended.

Davy cursed like he had heard Pa do once, and he leapt to his feet brandishing the crook.

But the night was quiet again, save for the pathetic moan of the sheep. He peered toward the woods, deep shadows of vastly tall trunks and stretching evergreen branches.

He had known better. The cottage was too close to the trees, and by refusing to move further afield, he had condemned the flock to greater risk of predators. Ghastwolves were not likely moving in large packs through the valley this time of year, but the occasional loner passed by as just demonstrated. Davy had known that. He, Davy ol'Sheffed, was a walking curse upon everything he touched.

He crouched by the injured sheep and tried to tend her wound, but it bled profusely, and she faded in front of him.

The dog whined.

"You did your job," Davy murmured, patting its head. "Keep watch."

Davy slit the sheep's throat like he had seen Pa do during culling, then tried parceling the meat out in logical pieces. He had no idea what he was doing.

The following days blurred together as Davy tried to survive, spending the days hoping the sheep wouldn't wander too far as he scrubbed and dried vegetables, attempted to make a fire, dried strips of mutton, and baked bread. He realized he had no yeast, and his bread came out dense and tasteless, as well as half-burnt.

It had to do.

Each evening he ushered the sheep to the protected cove by the lake. He took the horse everywhere. It was easier given how much he had to move, but it worked the horse harder and put her at risk during the night.

Back and forth, back and forth, with the nights becoming ever more chilly and the days becoming ever shorter.

He lost several more to the wolves, sometimes one and sometimes two. The attacks would often be accompanied by the distant roar of dragons and occasionally the heavy pressure of nearby wings as the massive creatures soared over the herd. There was little Davy could do besides smashing out with his crook, screaming curses, and siccing the dog on whatever threats he heard in the shadows.

Davy hated how everything he had loved in life had become an endless chore with no end in sight. He hated how alone he was, and then he began to hate the ol'Campens for pushing him away.

For having the Mark? Did it really matter? An angry, quiet voice inside told him it did, repeating its condemnation of him over and over.

And then one day, a lone figure came traipsing along the narrow dirt track.

Davy watched the speck turn into a silhouette, which then turned into a man. The man waved as he got closer, and he turned off the dirt track to meet Davy in the meadow.

"Bright day, boy. I'm on my way to Lupine, but the way has been a bit slow and I could use a roof over my head. Do you know of any lodging nearby?"

Davy shook his head. "The town is back that way, sir."

The man nodded. "I hoped to make it further. Might your parents have an extra bed? I have coin for the trouble."

Davy warily examined the man. He looked like a traveler, with a road-weathered cloak and heavy boots. He carried very little, with a long dagger strapped to one side and a light satchel hanging from his shoulder. The brim of his hat looked useful for shedding rain. "No parents, sir, but you can stay the night I guess."

The man stuck a big hand out and gave him a friendly smile. "I'm Toarval, boy. And you? Davon ol'Sheffed, eh? Well I thank you, Davon."

Toarval followed him to the cottage, seeming surprised when Davy left him there and began to usher the sheep to their sleeping area.

"It's not safe enough here," Davy explained. "But you can sleep in the bed and eat some of the bread on the mantle. And there's some dried meat hanging over the fire, and some berries in the basket on the table." He almost didn't tell the big man Toarval about the berries, for he had worked very hard to forage them on the hillside the day before, but his focus was on the coin promised.

If Davy was kind to the man, hopefully Toarval would pay him generously for the hospitality. That money would help Davy buy things he needed to survive the winter. (How he would get to town while keeping the flock safe, he didn't know. He wasn't sure about a lot of things.)

"You'll be alright out there?" Toarval said, quizzically raising an eyebrow. He grunted. "If you insist …"

Davy was surprised when the man came out the next morning, tracking him down with a basket of fresh bread and potatoes.

"Boy, you're really out here alone?" Toarval asked, setting the basket down.

Davy nodded.

Toarval grumbled. "That'll never do. Boy like you ought to be playing, running errands and the like."

Davy shrugged.

Toarval broke the bread into chunks. "I thought that might be, given the state of the bread. I made you some fresh; I hope you don't mind. You have more flour stored up, don't you?" Toarval grimaced at Davy's quiet indication. "That's not enough to get through winter, you know, and it's filled with worms."

Davy shrugged again. His days and nights repeated in a depressing and discouraging litany, reaching a point where he didn't think too hard about surviving until spring. He was just trying to survive until tomorrow.

Toarval's grimace turned to a scowl as he watched Davy devour the chunk of bread.

A rumble of thunder interrupted them, and they both looked up the mountainside. Dark clouds churned high and to the north, bubbling over a saddle and into the valley.

Toarval tightened his cloak around himself with an exaggerated shiver, although the breeze from the coming storm hadn't reached them yet. "Looks like the weather is turning. Are you going to stay out here?"

"I have to, sir."

Toarval nodded slowly, then glanced back toward the cottage. "Can I get you anything else? A heavier cloak?"

"Don't have one, sir."

Toarval heaved a big sigh and unclasped his travel cloak, a thicker layer than anything Davy had, and laid it around Davy's shoulders. "Tell you what, boy. You borrow that for now, and I'll rest my weary legs another day or two from the road. Is that alright with you?"

Davy looked up at the big man with awe. "Thank you, sir."

Toarval patted his shoulder. "Least I can do. And it gives me a warm shelter, rather than face this nasty rain and cold. I'm in no hurry to get where I'm going, long as I get there."

The storm was quick and intense, driving billowing rainclouds down from the peaks and along the valley, drenching Davy and his flock with bitterly cold rain. It dissipated partway through the day, but the chill remained.

Davy huddled with his extra cloak wrapped tightly around him and wondered how Pa had done this for so many years.

Winter would be brutal. Even if he worked hard, it seemed hopeless. Even the dog seemed to agree as it huddled next to him, occasionally nosing him with a cold wet muzzle.

Toarval returned the next morning with more food and a friendly smile. "Would you like some relief, Davon? I don't know much about sheep or horses, but I could watch them if you need a break."

"Don't you need to move on, sir?"

They both looked up at the sky, which was grey and overcast.

"Maybe not yet," said Toarval. "Looks to be more threatening than yesterday."

Davy agreed. Whether the heavy-laden clouds culminated in a storm or not, he was happy to have a friendly face nearby. One who didn't know about his Mark.

So Toarval stayed another day, watching the flock while Davy meandered back to the cottage. Once there, he spied all of the chores that still needed done. He finished hanging the onions and garlic braids over the window, standing on the table to reach. He scrubbed the last pile of potatoes in the stream and laid them out to dry. He tried to split some of the wood Pa had laid out months ago. The maul was heavy, and he couldn't swing it the way Mikkel did. As it had so many times at the ol'Campen's, it turned to one side as it fell, thumping the wood and bouncing off. Davy tried again and again, splintering a few chunks apart, but the wood pile was much smaller than he likely needed. The ol'Campens had twice this amount of firewood when he had left, thanks to Mikkel's hard work.

When he finally gave up, he re-entered the cottage and sat on the bed. The straw-stuffed mattress still had only the single fur and no blankets, but he lay down fully dressed and closed his eyes.

It had been weeks since he had been able to sleep without the nagging worry of the flock. He yawned wide and stretched, then curled into a ball and slept.

He didn't mean to sleep so long.

When he stirred, the Eye was already touching the highest tips of the western range.

Davy forced himself up, bleary-eyed and guilty. Toarval was probably wondering where he was, and probably hungry. Probably regretting his decision to help out.

He pulled the door shut with a bang and hurried downvalley, praying the predators had stayed away from Toarval. He broke into a run as dusk rushed onward, until he was forced to slow to avoid tripping. When he arrived at the meadow he had left that morning, his breath caught in his throat.

The flock was nowhere to be seen. No horse grazed among them, and no tall man wearing a hat and a traveler's cloak stood watch.

Davy squinted in the darkening evening, straining his eyes in every direction for a speck of white, but he saw nothing.

Could the ghastwolves have returned in number?

He shuddered at the memory of carnage, but there was no sign of that either. The meadow was devoid of any signs of conflict.

Dragons could have done it though, lifting their prey with a swoop and carrying them off to the heights.

Davy latched onto that idea, trying to avoid the darkest thought that nudged at him.

The flock had been stolen.

Davy swayed at an impasse as the last orange stripes of light beamed between the lowest peaks, and night settled in.

Should he search blindly in the dark? Maybe Toarval had simply brought them to a different meadow. Should he return to the cottage? For what? Toarval had his horse and crook. He had even taken his cloak back that morning since he was going to be sitting for so long.

Davy decided. He would search.

It was possible Toarval was lost or injured. He had said he didn't know much about herding. If a sheep had wandered too far, it was possible Toarval had not been successful trying to gather the stray up.

Davy stumbled along, heading further down the valley by the frail light of the quick moon, which was waning thin. After tripping several times, he found a long stick and used it as a cane.

But the next hill revealed no flock, nor the next, nor the next.

However, he did find the dog, its head a bloody mess. He knelt beside it. Dark splatters covered the grass where it lay, and its skull was bludgeoned to an odd shape on one side. Davy reached for a nearby rock, which was dark with dried blood. It slipped from his hand and rolled away.

"You were a good boy," Davy whispered, caressing the dog's cold muzzle. He felt sick to his stomach. Anger and guilt and sadness churned about inside, jumbled together with doubt and uncertainty. There could still be an explanation. Maybe the dog was hurt, and Toarval had put it out of its misery. Maybe someone else had come to steal the flock, and Toarval and the dog had chased after them. After all,

Davy had been friendly to Toarval, so surely the man would pay him in kind. That was how life worked.

He neared the ol'Campen's in the middle of the night. Their house was dark, and he spied the white specks in a distant field where either Mikkel or Mr. ol'Campen stood watch. Maybe they had seen something.

He pounded on the door, begging someone to answer, and someone did.

Tara flung the door open. "Davy, you're okay," she managed before her mother yanked her inside.

Mrs. ol'Campen blocked the doorway. "You can't be here, boy."

"My sheep are missing, ma'am," he stuttered. "Please, have you seen them?"

"No, now get ye far from here." Mrs. ol'Campen shut the door in his face.

He heard hushed arguing on the other side. Tara seemed to be speaking up for him, but the door remained shut.

Eventually he wandered further down the road that led from their log home toward the town, bypassing the distant ol'Campen flock by a wide margin.

He wanted to sleep, but he wanted to know even more whether the animals he cared for were alive. Pa's legacy. Davy's responsibility.

But there was no sign of them, and he reached the edge of town as the first dim signs of dawn appeared to the east.

Exhausted, he stumbled to the door of Ms. ol'Lannery where he curled up with a defeated sob. Pa would be so ashamed, and Ma would be disappointed.

He fell asleep tasting blood on his lip where he gnawed, but he hardly noticed compared to the ache in his heart.

7

Ms. ol'Lannery didn't happen to open her door to any customers that morning, and Davy remained curled in a heap in the shadow of her door.

Finally, he stumbled up, staggering further into town with his direction as muddled as his mind.

He passed the tavern, which was quiet, and paused only when the delicious whiff of pastries tickled his nose.

With bleary eyes, he glanced up to the bakery. The hefty baker, always a friendly man, poked his head out the door. "What are you in town so early for, boy?" The man put two flour-covered hands on his wide hips and looked Davy up and down with growing dismay. "You look like you haven't slept. Have a seat inside."

Davy followed the man in and sat in a wooden chair in front of the pastries. Their sweet, cakey scent wafted under his nose, and his stomach grumbled.

He dug through his coin purse. It was all he had, but he had to eat, right? He offered a quarter-mark with a trembling hand.

The baker swept it from his hand and replaced it with a crumbling handpie sprinkled with cinnamon and sugar. "You like those best, right, boy?"

"Sir?" Davy begged the man to stay, although he could see a glimpse of impatience as the man glanced at the steaming oven. "Can I work for you?"

The baker slowly knotted his brow and then excused himself to remove the next loaves of bread. "Not a lot of employment here, son. I can't make do if I pay another worker. And you're a bit short for the ovens."

"I can forage mushrooms and berries for you," Davy insisted, his voice going high with desperation. "I can make the daily stew for the bread bowls and make dough, and I'll do my best to split wood for the fire."

"Don't trust anyone to make my dough," laughed the baker, shoving a new batch of raw loaves into the oven. "Why aren't you at home with your flock?"

Davy broke down and cried where he sat, and a grimace crossed the baker's face.

"Come now, boy, you're scaring the other customers away," he grumbled. "I can't give you a job, okay? Crying ain't going to change that."

Davy tried to explain, but the baker had gotten a sour look and didn't seem to be listening. Instead he was intent on kneading his next batch of bread and smiling at incoming customers. When Davy finished his handpie, the baker ushered him out. "Go on now, go back home."

Davy tripped on a stone in the street. He kicked at it, but it was well-embedded in the ground and instead he stubbed his toe.

He wandered toward the smithy. The man was outside, sharpening a pile of knives from different customers on a spinning whetstone that he pumped with his foot.

Empathy filled the man's grimy face as Davy approached, and he paused his work. "Sorry to hear about your ma, boy. Thought you were staying with the ol' Campens now." The last words were almost a question, and the smith raised a quizzical eyebrow.

Davy bit his lip and climbed the short stone fence that surrounded the smith's outdoor work area.

"They made me leave." He couldn't explain why, for the smith might push him away too. "Can I have a job, sir?"

The smith set his work down and stood, a burly man with hefty shoulders, but not too tall.

If Davy worked hard, maybe he could become strong like the smith although he wasn't tall either. He could learn, and eventually he'd be muscular like Mikkel, right?

"Where's your flock?"

Davy held out his empty hands. "This is all I have, sir."

The smith pulled his lips to one side in a look of consternation, then clucked with disapproval. "I don't have much to spare, boy, sorry."

His wife came out. "Much spare?" She looked Davy up and down with curiosity, her eyes pausing on his swinging feet, and her face hardened as she recognized him. "No, we don't have anything to spare for boys with bad luck."

The smith's cheeks reddened, but he didn't argue with his wife.

Davy began to feel desperation eating at the fringes of his hope. "Sir, even a half-penny would help. Or a place to sleep?"

The smith snorted. "You want a handout?"

"No, sir. I'll work for it."

"Ain't got no work for a scrawny kid. You can't even work the bellows." The smith turned away and sat at his wheel, immediately setting it to a loud scraping turn that halted conversation. His wife crossed her arms and glared at Davy.

Davy blinked, trying to understand. The smith had been so kind before, as had the baker. What had changed? As far as Davy could tell, the only thing that had changed was himself. He was Marked. Everyone around him was damned by affiliation. His parents were dead. His flock was gone.

Perhaps the smith's wife was right to condemn him.

Did she know about the Mark? There was no way she could know already. Then he recalled the last time he had been to the smith, when he had mentioned his lame horse. Both smith and his wife had been troubled enough to pull out a black magic spell before finishing the shoeing. Davy really was bad luck, and no amount of hard work would make the smith think his presence worth the risk.

He examined his toes, hidden beneath boots that were a little too large. Then he scooched off the stone fence and shuffled away, wandering back the way he had come.

The seamstress waved at him through her open door with a generous smile. "Did your ma like her gift?" she inquired.

Davy twiddled his fingers and stared at his boots. "She never saw it, ma'am, but I left it on her grave."

The seamstress's smile tightened, then faded. "I didn't realize..." She cleared her throat. "Sorry, boy. What was your name again?"

"Davon, ma'am. My Pa and Ma always called me Davy."

She looked him up and down, then nodded to herself. "You're needing some help."

It wasn't a question, but Davy nodded anyway.

The seamstress took such a large breath through her nose, her nostrils flared. Then she waved him into the shop. "I can't help you much, Davy, but there's room for you to sleep in the back, if you help me with some errands here and there."

Davy nodded eagerly and thanked her.

All seemed like it would be well enough for a few weeks. The weather turned wet and volatile, sending several rainstorms through the village to muddy the streets, but Davy had a warm, dry place to rest every night, curled up amongst the bolts of dyed fabric and stacks of folded inventory.

Davy did everything he could to help the seamstress, who called herself Widow ol'Diran. Davy ran to the well for water, got her scissors sharpened at the smithy, and occasionally carried her wares to customers' homes. Most often, he ran to Ms. ol'Lannery's for new bolts of wool cloth and bundles of yarn.

Ms. ol'Lannery had changed too, using a brisk and unfriendly tone he had never heard her use with Ma. She never welcomed him in anymore, keeping their business strictly business. It made something inside Davy ache even more than the rejection by the baker or the smith. Ms. ol'Lannery had known him in his previous life; she had known his Ma and Pa. Yet, she treated him coldly with a brusque manner, as though she wanted him to leave her home as quickly as possible each time he stopped.

Winter settled over the town, covering the streets with a permanent layer of slushy muck.

Davy occasionally saw Mrs. ol'Campen or Tara come into town, and he imagined how his own valley was likely covered in a pristine layer of snow. He recalled the clear icicles that would form on the eaves, dripping and freezing till they were long enough for Pa to snap off and give to Davy.

He wondered if he would see his valley ever again, or if this new life was the only life he had to look forward to.

Once, Tara saw him from a distance and waved her arm, drawing his attention with desperate shouts. Her mother had grabbed her arm and marched away, leaving Davy awkwardly waving back at no one.

Widow ol'Diran was kind, giving him a bedroll and even sewing him a new ragdoll that looked like a sheep, but she had no spare food or clothing. Davy had spoken back once about how many cloaks she had stored in her inventory, but she had immediately bemoaned the necessity of selling her wares, not giving her talents away for free. Then she chastised him for being so selfish. He had felt guilty for asking afterward.

He ran out of money halfway through winter. He had used it to buy bread at the baker and hadn't wasted it on candy, but still the purse got lighter and lighter until one day, it was empty.

He stumbled through two days of hunger, laboring from one end of town to the other as he ran errands, before he realized how delicious the scones in the baker's window *really* looked.

They were pocked purple with kiltberries and drizzled with a sugary glaze, and they sat in a carefully arranged stack on a platter by the bakery door. They made his mouth water, and he licked his lips as he recalled Tara's delicious honey and Mrs. ol'Campen's jam.

Davy casually stepped into the bakery, as he had so many times before, and glanced around as though he were shopping. The baker ignored him, catering to other wealthier customers first as he knew Davy would likely buy a loaf of cheap, plain bread. No money for tangy caramels, cinnamon-filled sweet rolls, or road-worthy fruit cakes.

For once, being invisible was a blessing, and Davy inspected the shelves and platters quietly. Hearing the baker exchanging money and chattering with someone, he stuffed three scones into his shirt and shuffled out.

His heart raced as he nearly ran down the street to hide in an alley, where he scarfed one of the sweet, dense chunks. The crumbs were everywhere, glued to the inside of his shirt by frosting, and he greedily sucked on the fabric to get it clean. The sweet sugar mixed with salty sweat and dirt, but that didn't stop him. His hands were shaking, and he decided to eat one more to abate the hunger gnawing at his stomach.

Every bitter day after brought new temptations and challenges. He was starving, but he could only steal occasionally to avoid suspicion. He stole from the baker, the tavern, the street market that came together every few weeks, and other businesses whose owners he didn't know. He explored the other ends of town, finding new places with unfamiliar faces; hopefully they wouldn't recognize him either. Then he began to steal from windowsills and yards, sneaking into root cellars and smokehouses. He tried to be careful, but the baker began berating him for even entering the shop. The tavernkeeper's wife chased him out with a broom, calling him words he had never heard before.

And then one day, the seamstress stopped him before he headed out. "Davy, I've heard some things about town. Now I don't take much to gossip, but people have started to complain about you working for me."

Davy looked at his shoes and bit his lip guiltily.

Widow ol'Diran pursed her lips and gave him a stern look over her small spectacles, which hung from the bridge of her nose. "Whatever it is you're doing, stop it now. You'll bring a bad reputation to my store."

"Yes, ma'am," he said obediently.

But the taste of blood on his lip reminded him that he hadn't eaten anything for three days, that his stomach seemed to be eating itself in a continuously painful churning and grumbling.

What was he supposed to do?

Widow ol'Diran shooed him out. "Get on to Ms. ol'Lannery then. She ought to have two or three balls of white yarn for me by now, and perhaps even some new thread."

Davy wandered to the spinster's home and knocked. She didn't answer, and he knocked again. "Ms. ol'Lannery?" he called over the piercing wind that howled through the streets. He shoved his cold hands back into his pockets and glanced around.

Maybe she was out, or maybe she was bringing a hot snack to her hands in the back fields.

And maybe the door was unlocked.

He tried it, and the door swung open. The wind slammed it in with a bang.

Davy stepped inside and shoved it closed again.

Ms. ol'Lannery was nowhere to be seen, but a plate of sausages sat on the table. Their fatty scent tickled his nose and beckoned him over. He took one and shoved it in his mouth, savoring the juicy richness as it slid down his throat. He ripped a hunk out of the loaf of bread too before looking around again.

The house had a mixture of homey and business items, intermixed like the spinster's entire lifestyle. He spied her spinning wheel near a window and her loom in the next room, surrounded by baskets of apples and cards of wool and teacups on tiny plates.

"Ms. ol'Lannery?"

Hearing nothing, he wandered further inside. He passed a large barrel of potatoes and shoved as many as he could into his pockets.

Near the spinning wheel was a basket of loose yarn, but none prepared in balls for sale. He looked more closely. The wool texture was exceedingly fine, with a slightly brown undertone. His glance wandered to the wool she was using. It was familiar. She was working wool from their flock.

A pang of sadness stabbed into him, and he sat at the wheel with a huff.

This was all that remained. He fingered the half-formed yarn strung taut on the wheel. Then he looked out the window toward Ms. ol'Lannery's back pasture.

The woman appeared over a rise in a hill, trudging her way from the flock in the distance. It was larger than he remembered, and he squinted at the distant creatures.

Most of them looked white against the white snow, as Ms. ol'Lannery's flock had always been, but a few had dark brown faces and spackled legs that contrasted with the snow.

Davy stared as the woman got closer and closer. Then his eyes narrowed.

Those were his sheep.

By the time Ms. ol'Lannery reached the back door, Davy could feel the heat of anger burning through his entire body.

He met her at the door and stabbed a finger at the pasture. "Those are mine." He meant for it to come out strong and confident, but the highness of his voice betrayed him. Instead it was a whine, eked out by a poor, homeless boy. Nonetheless, he jutted his chin forward and tried to stand straight.

Ms. ol'Lannery paused in the doorway, then glanced over her shoulder at the distant flock. With a deep breath that raised her entire chest, she stepped into him and drove him backward, then shut the door. The expression on her face was colder than the howling wind outside, and he stumbled backward as she advanced.

He fell onto his rear with a yelp, but that didn't abate his anger. Instead the anger shifted from hot blushing and a pounding heart to burning tears that coursed down his cheeks. "Those are mine," he repeated.

"Those are mine, boy, and no one will question me about that. I've raised sheep for decades." She stepped over him and sat at the kitchen table as though they were having a friendly conversation.

"I can tell by what they look like," Davy replied. "I know what each one of them looks like."

"If that were true, surely it wouldn't have been so easy to lose them," said Ms. ol'Lannery with a wicked smile. She leaned forward. "And besides, I heard about more than your carelessness."

Davy cringed where he sat on the floor. Ms. ol'Lannery did always have the gossip of the town.

She had been Ma's biggest source of information. What did she know? That he was stealing?

"I know the ol' Campen's rid themselves of you for a reason." She seemed to enjoy that revelation, savoring the gossip with a lick of her chapped lips. "I know you're cursed, Marked. Who would have believed it? But then all those terrible things happened to your family." She clucked her tongue. "Your poor father, he never deserved such an end. And your mother, she must have known her death would be more merciful than the punishment of raising a Marked boy."

Davy's heart stilled completely, and he felt as though he were frozen to the floor. She knew.

She stabbed her fork into a sausage and bit into it with a smacking sound. "If you try to say anything about my sheep, I'll tell everyone you've been Marked."

Davy trembled, and his voice came out timid and quiet this time. "Please don't."

Ms. ol' Lannery bared her teeth in a semblance of a grin. A bit of parsley stuck between her teeth. "It would be such a shame for you to lose the goodwill of Widow ol' Diran, when you have so little else. What does she need today, by the way?"

Something flickered inside Davy in that moment. Something that changed his self-pity and heavy shame into something else: hatred.

He had nothing because he had no one. Because the world had taken and taken and taken, dragging and raking at his skin til it was raw and bloody. He had nothing because everyone who should have helped him had chosen themselves over him, stolen from him, and battered him into the muddy streets with the heel of their boots.

And maybe he deserved it, because he was Marked and had brought evil to his own family.

Maybe he had never worked hard enough to compensate for his inborn shortcoming.

Maybe he didn't deserve better.

Or maybe he did, but people were cruel and terrible. Maybe they were worse than ghastwolves or Earth Dragons or the dark terror of tragic deaths like Pa's.

He scrambled to his feet to face Ms. ol'Lannery. "Those are my sheep," he said again. This time, it didn't sound like a whine, although his voice was still just a boy's.

Ms. ol'Lannery seemed unaffected. "You really are Marked, aren't you? It's not just a rumor." Before he could stop her, she had grabbed at him and spun him around, then forced his tunic up.

Potatoes fell from his pockets as he struggled against her, but he was too small to resist her solid grip. She stretched the skin on his back and cackled. "By the Light, it is true." She shoved him away. "And you've stolen from me. I owe you nothing, boy." She grabbed him by the collar and dragged him to her front door, then tossed him into the street.

He landed in a heap, scraping a hole through his pant knee and sloshing mud into his boots.

Ms. ol'Lannery chuckled a cruel, slow chuckle, then slammed her door shut.

He nursed his knee for minutes as he realized all that had happened. Ms. ol'Lannery, the biggest gossip in town, knew his secret. The ol'Campens must have let it slip, and now she had leverage over him to hold his lips sealed about his sheep.

His entire flock wasn't there in her back pasture though, of that he was sure. Toarval must have taken some of them somewhere else. Was Toarval truly a traveler passing through? Had he taken most of the flock elsewhere, or was he still linked to the village somehow?

Davy trudged back to Widow ol'Diran's shop slowly, favoring his bleeding knee and empty-handed of her woolen yarns.

If she found out about his Mark, she would abandon him too. Apparently love *depended*.

He gnawed on his lip as he tried to think of excuses for why he had failed in his errand, but he couldn't think of anything.

He skirted the tavern on the far side of the street, and as expected the tavernkeeper's wife stepped up to the glass window and watched him pass with a leery eye.

Maybe Toarval would show his face in town, if Davy paid close enough attention. He decided this was the best course of action as he arrived at his temporary home and scufffed his muddy boots on the doormat.

"Did Ms. ol'Lannery not have the yarn ready?" asked the seamstress without looking up from her work.

Davy mumbled a noncommittal sound.

She sent him on a different errand, although she seemed somewhat annoyed and hadn't noticed the hole in his trousers.

Davy reiterated to himself. *Love depends.*

With a frustrated, resentful huff, he headed back out to the horrid windstorm, which was starting to drop a freezing sleet that made everything slippery.

He continued on this way, working as hard as he could for the seamstress but sensing an icy chasm opening between them. More and more often, the people to whom she sent him for errands would slam the door in his face. They would get a strange look, and their eyes would go from curious to distant and neutral. And he would fail to do what Widow ol'Diran needed him to do, and he would return with wet boots and freezing fingers with nothing gained.

"Why couldn't you deliver it?" she snapped one day, snatching his parcel meant for the tavernkeeper from his hands.

He shook his head. "They wouldn't listen."

In truth, the tavernkeeper had caught Davy not two days earlier rummaging through the scraps dumped behind his shop. That had been the last straw for the tavernkeeper, who declared Davy a "damned bothersome harassment who made his business look bad, loitering like he did." Davy didn't know what "harassment" or "loitering" meant, but it sounded bad. Now Davy was afraid to approach the tavern for fear his dirty rags and muddy boots and impoverished demeanor would sully the man's doorstep. But he still had errands to complete, and he didn't know how to do so and please Widow ol'Diran.

Widow ol'Diran pursed her lips, an expression she seemed to do more and more frequently, and stomped to the backroom. She returned with his bedroll in hand and tossed it out the door into the muddy slush on the street. "You can keep that, but you can't stay here anymore. I know what you are, and I can't have my livelihood ruined by your curse."

"But ma'am—" he stuttered. How could she know? Unless Ms. ol'Lannery had told her, which she probably had done. The spinster did nothing but spin stories and wool all day.

"Everyone knows, boy. How could you lie to me, bringing that kind of evil into my home? You're a selfish little mongrel, and I'm done with you." The seamstress shoved him out the door and slammed it behind him.

Davy noticed numerous passersby glance at him with sour looks, their faces pinched against the cold and their cheeks flushed. They all hurried by without a word, and one of them stepped in a puddle that further soaked his bedroll.

Davy gathered the sopping blanket in his arms, sniffling a little as the cold seeped through his jacket.

Love depended. It depended on whether the other person had something to gain or lose, and on whether it was easy. Love depended on convenience.

That much he knew now.

He scurried to the next warm place he could think of, a pigsty on the edge of town that had a closed area for the young ones. And that was where he slept, enduring the bitter night which he hoped was the last harsh breath of winter.

8

The days grew longer, and the white sun stretched a little further with a bit more heat.

Davy hid most of the time, nestling between the warm but rough bodies of the pigs and eating their slop and occasionally venturing to nearby root cellars to steal potatoes and carrots. Whenever the owners came out to feed the pigs, he would scuttle under the loose hay mounded in the corner, praying they wouldn't notice him.

Sometimes he snuck out to find more food, but many of the townspeople kicked at him or yelled for him to get away. They would make signs to I'ya and mutter a prayer, or they would spit to one side for good luck. Others cringed and turned their faces away as though he carried some contagion. Ms. ol'Lannery had fulfilled her position as town gossip well, assuring her own safety and future. She would have the best wool in town forever.

From his pigsty, Davy watched.

Situated on the edge of town, his view through the cracked boards of the sty gave him a vantage point toward the town's western entry road, which he scanned with suspicious, narrowed eyes anytime a traveler passed by. He watched for Toarval, and for any sign of the rest of his flock or horse.

The air stopped clawing at his lungs and sapping his toes, and traffic into town developed the rhythm of spring. Market days resumed, and Davy watched especially close.

And then it happened.

Toarval, wrapped in a dyed woolen shawl, marched into town from the west carrying a laden knapsack, a thick beard and contented smile upon his face. His boots were fine leather, and he stepped confidently with the assistance of a shepherd's crook.

Not Pa's crook though. A different one, one that was a little taller and knobbier, made of a different pine with unique knots and carving.

Toarval's hooded cloak was pulled up to keep him comfortable in the early spring chill, and he wore a tawny woolen cap on his head.

Davy sucked a breath in as he peered through the crack in the pigsty.

The man trudged by, oblivious to the presence of the boy from whom he had taken everything, and continued into town.

Davy stole out from the sty, intent on confronting Toarval, but then realized maybe he should only follow, maybe take whatever was in the man's knapsack. Maybe he could snatch the coin purse hanging from Toarval's belt, a recompense for what the man had taken.

Toarval gave a friendly wave to the smith as he passed by.

"How's the family, sir?" called the smith.

"Well," Toarval returned. "I appreciate the loaned axehead this last month. I can repay you today."

"A village does what it can for each other, sir. It's no hassle." The smith nodded respectfully, and Toarval tipped his woolen cap.

"I'll catch you on my return," Toarval assured him.

"Happy to hear your family's well, after such a hard season last year."

Toarval tipped his cap again and continued on.

Davy scurried after him, hiding behind building corners and stacked boxes and carts. Toarval knew the smith? Then his story of being a traveler was indeed a lie. Who was he then?

Toarval entered the butcher shop to the music of the tinkling door bell, and Davy rushed up to the window to peer inside. He couldn't enter, not without being yelled at.

"Toarval, my friend," the butcher said in greeting. "Here for the sausages?" He wiped a hand shining with slick fat on his apron.

"Yes, sir," Toarval replied, shaking the man's hand. "You said you're willing to resale most of it?"

"Aye, it'll fetch a fine price here in town." The butcher disappeared into his backroom and returned with an armful of wrapped meats. He hefted them onto the counter.

Toarval packed them carefully into his knapsack as the butcher counted out a pile of coins.

"Less the value of that sausage," muttered the butcher while tabulating, "here's the full sale of your mutton. Good quality tender meat too; I kept some back for roasts, smoked 'em. Culls aren't normally that young."

Toarval made an agreeable sound and cleared his throat, then counted the money into his purse. "Much appreciated, sir. I can't say enough how helpful you were these last months. My family will be back on its feet with I'ya's blessing."

"You're part of a community now, sir. I myself am relieved to have such a fine family come into the area. You know, my son is but a year or two older than your daughters."

"That brawny lad who helped us cull?" Toarval gave the butcher a winning smile. "I think both girls were winking at him by the end of the day. Their mother was quite distraught."

Both men chuckled at that.

"Well, perhaps you ought to bring the elder into town next market day, and I'll make sure my boy works the front." The butcher stuck out a hand once again.

"I'll do that," said Toarval, shaking the man's hand in parting. "Bright morning to you."

"And you, sir."

Davy scrambled back to hide behind the corner as Toarval exited the shop.

The man patted his coin purse with satisfaction, then turned to walk down the street.

In his haste to follow, Davy stumbled into another pedestrian, who shoved him to the ground.

"Watch it, boy," grunted the man with a look of distaste.

Davy got up and rubbed his sore rear end. At least the road was dry today. He scuttled out of the way as another person walked by, shoving past him with a shoulder.

Finally regaining his bearings, he looked where Toarval had gone and spied the man at a busy wagon, the first wayfarer to pass through town. Several wayfarers, clearly a family, stood around the wagon, displaying a variety of wares and chattering with the growing crowd.

This was perfect. Davy could hide among the crowd til he was right next to Toarval, then relieve him of his coins.

His mouth watered with the thought of what he could buy with a quarter-penny or two.

And more than anything, he was certain the mutton sausage in Toarval's knapsack was made from Davy's flock. Toarval had lied. He was a herdsman, like Pa. Horror ran through Davy as a faint memory nagged. Ms. ol'Lannery had mentioned a family last year. A family with two fine daughters (one blonde and one dark, would you believe it?), who had lost a huge portion of their flock to Earth Dragons. A tragedy, to be sure. Davy had pitied them greatly, as the family had been forced to give up herding and move into town. Or had they? Toarval had recovered enough sheep to rebuild his flock, and what fine animals they were with that excellent wool and dark skin!

Davy slipped into the crowd, trying to be inconspicuous, and moved right behind Toarval. Toarval was negotiating with the wayfaring auntie, an elderly woman with grey braids and sun-wrinkled skin. The woman wheezed at him while displaying a pretty cotton skirt dyed a light sunny yellow and embroidered with brown flowers and swirls along the hem.

Davy tried to focus on the task in front of him, instead of the bitter thought that the skirt was for Toarval's eldest daughter, who was apparently pretty enough to catch the eye of the butcher's son. Such an alliance would strengthen both families, a shepherd with a well-bred flock and a butcher who could process the mutton. And all of that had developed since Toarval disappeared with Davy's sheep. No doubt the butcher had known the sheep he helped cull were from the ol'Sheffed bloodline, and he had ignored the fact for selfish gain.

Davy slipped his small knife from his belt and reached for the fat coin purse dangling in from him.

He managed to rip a hole in it, spying a glint of shining copper, when a powerful hand gripped his forearm like a vice.

"Thief," snarled Toarval, yanking him around so that his feet slipped out from under him. Toarval's eyebrows arched up for the briefest of moments as he recognized him, but the moment was fleeting, as ephemeral as love and kindness.

Davy's wrist bent in an odd direction as Toarval flung him about, and something twisted the wrong way. He cried out with the flaring pain, but no one seemed to hear him over the shouts of the crowd.

He heard someone call for the baron.

"The lord's away on business," he heard Ms. ol'Lannery say. "I saw him ride out a few days ago."

"Well, the boy ought to be punished."

"Can't punish without the baron's judgment."

"Ain't that the cursed boy?"

The crowd grew still at that, and Davy felt the burn of every eye upon him where he sat in the road, nursing his screaming wrist. He had dropped his knife.

"What do you mean, cursed?" said one woman in a shaky, fearful voice.

"The boy is Marked," declared Ms. ol'Lannery, her voice ringing with self-importance. "I've seen it myself."

The crowd backed away, with some nodding knowingly while others glanced about fearfully as if hoping their neighbor would refute the statement.

"You know, I had three pigs die this winter," said someone.

"I lost eight sheep to ghastwolves," said another. "That's far more than usual."

The crowd erupted into accusations and complaints of all the things that had gone wrong that winter.

"No," Davy cried. "I didn't cause any of that. I lost my sheep too, because he stole them from me." He pointed at Toarval.

Toarval feigned innocence, raising both hands as if Davy aimed a slingshot at him. "I don't know what you're talking about, boy. I've never seen you in my life." Toarval shook his head somberly at Davy, barely containing a triumphant smirk beneath his stiff, cold expression. Then he looked at Ms. ol'Lannery, his eyebrows raised with exaggerated fear. "You said he's Marked by evil?"

Ms. ol'Lannery declared the truth of it, and the crowd spoke over each other in a rising frenzy.

"My chimney caught fire last week, would have burnt the entire cottage had I not been there."

"My dear mother fell ill, still hasn't recovered."

"Our meat turned rancid, and our turnips went soft."

"The boy's brought all this upon us, I'm sure of it."

Davy looked wildly about. How could any of that be his fault? But the circle around him tightened, and he felt as though they might string him up at any moment and slit his throat like a cull.

"If he's Marked, he doesn't deserve a trial and judgment. He shouldn't even exist."

"The little varmint's been harassing my business for months, stealing scraps and scaring my customers."

"My breads and cakes have gone missing too many times," shouted the baker.

"I lost a cloak last month."

"Our root cellar was tampered with."

"Enough," declared Toarval, raising his hands to calm the crowd. "I think we all know what needs to be done. This creature stole from me and many of you, and must be handed over to the baron, but if our lord is out of town, we must detain him somewhere safe from the rest of us."

The crowd looked at each other.

"How about the old well?"

"He won't be able to get out. The Temple can bless it afterward if we really need it again."

Davy clutched the injured wrist close to his chest to protect it, and Toarval grabbed him by the other arm and yanked him along.

The mass migrated through the streets, jeering and hustling each other onward.

Only one small voice protested, a high, thin reed of a young girl. "Please, everyone, he did nothing to deserve this," cried Tara. She appeared next to Davy and tugged on Toarval's arm, but he brushed her off. She stumbled over her skirts, then hiked them up to continue forward. Tears streamed down her pale cheeks, the first empathy Davy had seen in weeks, maybe even months.

"Davy!" she cried. "Davy, there's nothing wrong with you."

It changed nothing.

Davy felt himself lifted over the stone lip of the abandoned well and dropped in.

He landed with a cold splash that sapped the fire from his muscles, and he flopped with a splash to the edge.

The well was unevenly chiseled from hard stone, partially bricked to fill in large divets but retaining a roughness from the town's attempt to break through stony soil.

Davy winced as he almost put weight on his sprained wrist, but managed to scramble halfway out of the water onto a narrow ledge. He panted with the effort, unsure whether the pain in his wrist was greater or lesser than the pain of rejection.

A scream from above made him glance up. "Davy!" Tara screamed, her face framed by the sky above. Then she was pulled away, and Davy heard her mother.

"He's a lost cause," declared Mrs. ol'Campen. "We're goin' home now."

"But he's family now. He's got no one else."

Davy heard the struggle above, and suddenly Tara appeared again with a sack in hand. She flung it down, and a few potatoes and berries splashed into the water.

"I'm sorry, Davy," she cried as someone pulled her away. Her protests and apologies were superseded by the creaking of wood as someone covered the well.

He cried, begging for mercy. His own high voice screamed at his eardrums as it reverberated off the walls. Then he shouted in anger, calling them all the names he had heard over the previous months. Ma would have been ashamed. Pa would have whipped him and washed his tongue with soap.

But no one listened, and he was left alone in the dark. The echoing slurs and curses that bounced down the walls faded away, and then disappeared. The intermittent shading of the cracks in the well cover by unknown curious bodies above halted, and the heavy silence of despair grew, filling the well and pushing the walls outward.

Realizing he really was alone, he turned to gathering the potatoes and berries from Tara's sack. He scarfed the berries immediately.

Finally, his throat hoarse and his body exhausted, he fell into a silent desperate prayer. Although love from others depended, maybe clemency from the highest power didn't. Maybe the great Eye could see through the tiny cracks of the wooden well cover.

Please, save me, he thought, clasping his fingers together over knobby, tucked-in knees. *Please. Even if I'm Marked, I want to live.*

9

THE NIGHT WAS TERRIBLY cold with wet feet, but Davy had endured worse the previous months.

Tucked in a tight ball of misery, he sat on the narrow ledge, trembling and missing the heat from the coarse-haired hogs with whom he normally slept.

Someone had tossed a loaf of bread down before dusk with a careless shout of warning. The bread had splashed into the water, but Davy had retrieved it quickly. The crusty outside had protected a surprising amount of the loaf from becoming soggy, not that such a state would have stopped Davy from eating it anyway. He shoved the entire thing down, unable to ration it out like he would have while shepherding.

There was no hope of tomorrow in any case.

With the flock, he had endured the difficult days and black nights with discipline knowing that he was the guardian of something else, something important. He protected the sheep, giving them safety and sleep and joyful grazing. Before that, he also protected his family's peace, helping Pa and Ma to maintain their beautiful livelihood. Such a quest was one worthy of a knight, he imagined, or at least a knightly man. And a knightly man guarding his family would ration his food and stay up all night on watch without a whisper of complaint.

If he had tears left, they would have slipped down his cheek. Instead, his young face pulled back in a wince at the painful memories and predictions for tomorrow.

He need not ration the bread or potatoes or berries because tomorrow might be his death. He had no family or flock to guard or care for, no friends who would miss him should he disappear, except for Tara. When the Baron returned, his judgment would likely be what the townspeople wanted: death, earned through a litany of sins including theft but foremost for being Marked.

Tara. She was the only one who didn't make sense in all of this. Everyone believed he was cursed and hated him for all the bad luck he had brought upon them, except her. Why? He didn't deserve love.

Davy hunched into another intense prayer. *Please take my Mark away. If you're there...* Maybe if it was gone, they could find mercy in their hearts for him. Maybe he could be loved like he so desperately needed.

The next day was the same, and the next. He could see the warm sunshine of early spring piercing through the cracks of the well cover, and he shifted on the ledge so that one of the tiny beams touched his skin. He couldn't climb out with his injured wrist, nor were there handholds higher up. The old well was an effective prison.

Someone threw another loaf of bread down, but then another person followed it with a rotten squash and jeering laughter. Davy shouted for help nonetheless, but received only silence in answer. He ate the bread, a welcome reprieve from the earthy crunch of raw potatoes.

As he finished it, he wondered why Tara had tried to help him. He wondered why someone else had thrown a loaf of bread down. Were there times when people cared without reason, when they defied the world of superstition and earned affection and loved anyways? Was it possible that his Mark was nothing more than a meaningless birthmark, that he could be worthy of love and life?

A strange sense of peace entered him. Despite knowing he would likely die soon from either starvation or execution, he had figured it out. His parents had refused to give him up knowing that he emerged from the womb as he was, and Tara had never once wavered from caring about him. And that was enough.

He buried his head one more time with a sigh. He might die, but he really didn't want to. *Save me, please, someone,* he prayed with hope as faded as the brown dye of his threadbare tunic.

From what?

The thought invaded his mind, and his head shot up to look around. The dark glass of the well's water was in front of him, still and unwavering. Far above, the wooden well cover remained in place.

Was it the voice of the Eye?

He clasped his hands together more tightly in supplication. *Please save me from this well,* he began, then faltered. *Save me from this life, from these people.*

People need to be saved from people? The voice was genuinely confused, ending its thought with a high intonation. Davy could imagine someone cocking their head and scrunching their eyebrows together.

He tried to pray earnestly, although he didn't understand how I'ya could not know his need, given how the Eye watched day after day after day. *Yes, sometimes people do things that don't make sense. I need help to get away. I need to start over, maybe go south.*

I do not know south, but I know "away," replied the voice. *Is south the same as away?*

Callendera was south, Davy knew. The Herding Master Hall was south. *Yes,* he answered, *I suppose south is the same as away for me.*

Why are you in a well?

Davy tried to explain. He felt more and more that the disembodied voice could not be I'ya, for the Eye would have seen all of the things he described happening to him.

So you are being punished for your crimes? Then I do not think I can help you. You should be punished for crimes committed because crimes are wrong.

The sliver of hope, as narrow as the sunbeam that tickled his skin, fizzled and deflated. Then the anger and frustration that had brewed in him all winter came out, and he shouted aloud. "Do you really think any of what I've done is wrong?"

The voice was silent for a while, and for minutes Davy was terrified that the spirit had gone. Then it finally spoke. *Your intentions were not evil, but your deeds were not just. Stealing is wrong.*

"That's not why they threw me in this well," Davy said sadly. "If they were worried about me stealing a few coins or food to survive, they would have branded me or cut my hand or put me in the stocks."

Then why?

Davy sniffled, wishing he could see whatever was speaking to him. "Because they believe I'm cursed." His whisper bounced off the well walls, coming back to his ears in a mocking echo.

Again, silence. Then, *I do not understand.*

"I'm Marked," whispered Davy, finally admitting it aloud although he didn't believe in it himself. "Marked means I deserve to die, although I don't think I do."

This does not seem right, said the voice. *I will help you.*

At first, Davy thought he imagined the dull, distant thunder. Then he thought maybe a spring storm was brewing, with tumbling black clouds that spilled down the mountainside and clashed into lightning and fat raindrops. The sound grew louder, and Davy thought he felt a quiver beneath his bony rear end, which was sore from sitting in the same position for so long.

He heard shouts of dismay from above, and he thought he heard his name as the shaking increased.

The earth was moving. Clods of dirt and rock crumbled from the side of the well, crashing into the water with a splash that wet Davy's legs. The surface, formerly serene, bounced and quivered with the upset, eventually coming to a loose pattern like a giant's footsteps.

The regular sound had direction, seemingly behind Davy, through the wall. He turned his head and placed his ear against the earth. It was a clawing, tearing sound, and it was escalating to a roar of dislodged rock and dirt.

I am almost there, said the voice in Davy's head just as he heard the creaking sound of the well cover. Light streamed down, and he heard the townspeople above shouting more clearly.

"By the Light, he's brought ruin upon us."

"The earth quakes like an avalanche. My shed might fall over."

"We are cursed now, just like the ol'Sheffeds."

Davy jumped back as the earth next to his ear crumbled apart to a violent crash, and he fell into the water with a startled cry. When he resurfaced, sputtering, he clutched for the ledge and gasped when he smacked his sore wrist on the rock. He grabbed on with his other hand and found a warm muzzle under his fingers. It pulled him out as he hung on, and then he came face to face with a creature with magnificent whirling rubies for eyes.

They both stared at each other, entranced, and the chaos above faded away.

Davy found his hand still on the creature's muzzle: a predator's snout, somewhat shorter like a bear rather than a wolf, with gleaming blades for fangs. It had no ears, but it did have a blood-red soft mane that started on the top of its head and went down its neck like a horse. Its front legs were stout and thick with bulky claws like a badger. The warm skin under Davy's fingers was scaled like a snake, and each piece glimmered with a rainbow of crimson and burnished oranges.

"You're beautiful," he managed in a soft voice that seemed over-loud in the echoing well.

And all at once, a new sense of joy exploded into his being. It rushed irresistibly from his tattered heart to his limbs, shivering through his extremities until his fingers tingled. It exploded through his head til he was dizzy, like spinning around in endless circles until he landed in the valley's lush grass. It leapt from his throat like laughter and opened his eyes.

It wasn't an *it*. It was a she, and she was everything.

Her gemstone eyes danced, fixed entirely on his while melding from color to color, and he knew she felt the same. He couldn't explain it, and he couldn't stop it.

I did not expect to find you, she said, emphasizing the last word with awe. *Not after so long alone. I am Ar'we.*

"I'm Davon."

Their moment was interrupted by angry shouts from above.

"He's summoned a monster!" someone cried.

"Kill them both. We can't wait for the lord!"

Then a rock sailed down and smacked Ar'we in the head. She snarled upward, ignoring the sudden red gash that blossomed. Davy yelped as something hit his head as well.

Follow me now, Ar'we said, vanishing backward into her tunnel.

Another brick smashed down, hitting Davy's outstretched fingers, and he yelped again. He heard Ar'we hiss as he threw himself into the darkness after her.

Davy stumbled down the tunnel, quickly losing the dim light from the open well. The bottom was wet with groundwater, and he slogged through it, feeling the damp get into his worn boots at the soles.

"Ar'we, wait," he called blindly, but he immediately tripped over something. He realized it was her tail, a long tapering thing that flicked lightly in his searching hand. "May I?" He held onto it as she guided him through the eternally black night of a tunnel system beneath his own world. It was considerably warmer, except for the thick muck on the bottom. The air was rich with fertile soil and dusty rock, heavily-laden with a heat that seemed to come from the bowels of the earth.

He and Ar'we didn't speak aloud, as he was already stretching his body's strength in order to keep up with her. He could hardly keep his breath, having been malnourished and mistreated, and his wrist ached terribly. He had to make sure he didn't use it to catch himself if he tripped.

Nevertheless, they communicated. His thoughts were of gratitude and joy and wonder, and hers were of relief and comprehension. They mixed like two thunderous rivers joining in springtime, a violently unstoppable melding til the two couldn't be separated again. Their thoughts then churned and tumbled into their past, the time before this bond. His thoughts were of Ma and Pa and heartbreak and betrayal, and hers were of an almost unendurable period of desperation and loneliness. She was young, like him, and simultaneously *not*, for she had been out of her egg for many painful years longing for this connection without hope. Like the others, she assumed she would not find him before the time of bonding was over, and she would be alone for a very long time. She hadn't rescued him expecting to bond with him; she had merely been curious about the mental cries of anguish she heard.

"There are others?" he managed. They had slowed down somewhat now that they were far from the town, and he could tell they were steadily ascending. His panting had shifted to exhausted wheezing huffs.

Ar'we affirmed there were. *We will be to a safe place soon.*

Davy imagined the abyss ahead of him lightening to a warm red of a hearth, a well-tended fire flickering over hardwood. He imagined the walls of their tunnel appearing, so he could reach out and touch them, feeling their grainy crumble of earth and broken roots. He imagined the moment the warm tail, slick with incredibly smooth scales, would finally show itself in the dim glow, and he could take in the wonder of Ar'we once more.

He blinked a few times, realizing that time had come.

Ar'we's sinuous tail extended up to her rump, which swung ahead of him as she stomped from paw to paw. Her back legs were shorter, powerful with thick toes for shucking the earth aside. As the tunnel they were in opened up to a dimly lit cavern, he could see her entire body. Her flowing mane extended down her back to her tail tip, and all of her seemed to glow with radiant heat, her scales reflecting the tiniest bit of light with a scarlet iridescence. Her forelegs were stout as well.

He had never seen a creature like her before, but he knew nothing would ever be as perfect in his sight as her.

Ar'we led him toward an opening on the other side of the cavern, which boasted the cool light of the waning day.

This is our home, she said simply as she led him to the last cave.

Davy's eyes took a moment to adjust as he stepped into an even larger cavern, which had a blindingly bright opening to outside on the far end. Massive shapes emerged from the corners of the room and descended on him, encircling him with a torrent of whispered thoughts. His courage failed, and he scurried forward from Ar'we's tail to hide between her forelegs. She paused and curled her tail around, forming a barrier between him and the other creatures. His scrawny back pressed against the heat of her core, and he felt her projecting a sense of comfort to him.

Unlike her, these creatures were known. They stalked forward on bent forewings, crouching down to peer at him with their keen predator eyes and baring their dagger-sized teeth. Strangely, he didn't perceive aggression or hunger, but rather a bland curiosity.

You've bonded with a hamanool, said one, cocking its head to one side. *Praise the Light.*

Praise the Light, echoed several others.

Davy shook. Earth Dragons, the massive brutes who had ripped Pa away from him and yanked his sheep from under his care. Anger welled up, and having nothing else, Davy stooped and picked up a rock. He threw it at the nearest Earth Dragon with a furious shout. "You're the reason Pa died," he screamed. "You Earth Dragons, you're monsters. Go away!"

A jarring sense of sadness invaded him, and he turned to see Ar'we staring at him. Her eyes had turned cold with fright and shame, like a faded pink rose after the first frost. She didn't speak, instead backing up slightly and folding her foreleg knuckles under. The talons shifted and distended, with a web of skin stretching out between them taut and thin. The foreleg adjusted, lengthening along one bone and shortening on the other. Her powerful digging claws had disappeared, replaced by wings like he had seen all his life on the distant predators on the peaks. She was one of them.

You think I am a monster? she asked in a tone that indicated she already knew the answer.

Davy trembled where he stood and clenched a second rock in his hand. Confusion threatened to overwhelm him as he spun from Ar'we to the others, who were much larger and frightening than she. They all watched him, their eyes whirling and glowing in the failing light.

The one he had thrown a rock at already caught his gaze. *Child of I'ya, we are the daragool of the Sikrat Mountains, and we are far from mindless beasts.*

"But you attacked my Pa. I saw it happen." Davy's voice shook and cracked, and he found himself crying at the dark memories, of the flashes of red in the night and the gleam of teeth as a large dragon head swung over him that fateful night. He heard Ar'we whimper, and it ripped his heart in half.

The large dragon regarded him and cocked its head once again. *You were the boy in the valley.*

Bitterness filled Davy, and he fought against the desire to comfort Ar'we. He *was* right.

No, Child of I'ya. The voice was firm. *We tried to protect you.*

The second rock slipped from Davy's grip as he tried to comprehend the dragon's words.

There had been dragons every time a large ghast-wolf attack happened, but had he ever seen a dragon actually take a sheep? He admitted that he had not. Ms. ol'Lannery claimed dragons had killed most of Toarval's flock, but then again, Toarval was a liar, and so was Ms. ol'Lannery. Had Davy ever seen the distant creatures do anything more than soar over the valley and stretch their magnificent wings?

Wiping his tears with a filthy sleeve, he turned back to Ar'we. She slumped on the ground, her eyes dulled and tortured. She didn't look at him.

"I'm sorry," Davy whispered, and he closed the space between them. He wrapped his arms around her muzzle, placing his forehead against hers, and hugged her with all his strength.

Joy infused him as it burst from Ar'we. She crooned with happiness, sending a vibration through him like music. It danced through his veins and sang in his mind, and he knew in the deepest part of himself that he could never deny that song. Ar'we was with him forever, and he was with her. Her love would never *depend*, nor would his. No matter what trials they faced, what arguments they had, they were irrevocably together. He clutched Ar'we as tightly as he could, despite the ache in his wrist, and he kissed the tender spot on her skull where she had been struck earlier. He apologized for his blind anger, and he knew she had forgiven him already.

The tears that escaped now had a different flavor from those of the past three seasons. Was it possible for salt to taste any different? But it did. Instead of the harshness of bitter, lonely tears that slicked their way down his cheeks and curved into his dimples and leaked into his mouth, these tears flushed the scales of hate and anger from his eyes. They washed his heart clean and rinsed the dirt and shame away. They were cathartic, releasing him from the misery in which he had been drowning.

He tightened his hold on Ar'we, and she nuzzled him back, then wrapped her tail around him in an embrace. "We'll always be together?" he sniffled, still unable to believe it.

Ar'we projected pure ecstatic adoration.

Always.

Epilogue

Summertime was the best part of living in the high mountains. The sunshine made the glaciers beyond the cave entrance glitter in waves of eternal sparkles, and the tiny flowers that nudged from the dusty cracks bloomed, attracting tiny butterflies that moved in clustered groups.

One landed on Ar'we's nose, and another landed on her forehead. Two more fluttered onto her tail, touching her with delicate curled tongues as they explored the crevices between her scales. She suppressed a snort, not wanting to startle them away, and lay frozen on her vantage point overlooking the valley below.

Davy skipped up, a freshly picked flower crown in hand and a wide open-mouthed grin on his face.

I can't move, Ar'we warned, her nostril twitching. She crossed her eyes trying to focus on the butterfly tickling her nose. It slowly opened and closed its lavender wings.

Davy tiptoed closer and set the flower crown gently aside, then gazed over the high valley far below them. From here, he could see the lone horned bull that wandered across the marshy bottom, the family group of elk grazing in the sparse trees, and the river-barrower that scurried about packing more mud on its impressive dam. He could see his old cottage as a grey speck in the distance, but he had no desire to go to it. Somewhere in the green meadow, however, were two graves on which he and Ar'we would leave fresh flowers soon. He rubbed his arm; his wrist was nearly healed, his wounds forgotten and forgiven.

"Looks like we may have to stay here for a while then," he said softly, appreciating the lilac hue of the butterfly on Ar'we's muzzle. It flapped its wings ever so slowly as it absorbed the warm sunshine, and shortly another joined it with a flutter of purple and white.

Davy smiled.

Afterword

Please leave a review!

If you enjoyed the story of young Davon and Ar'we, please provide a review on Goodreads, Bookbub, or Amazon. Your words are powerful, and your support means the world to me. Something as simple as a star rating can make all the difference!

You can purchase a signed physical copy through R. M. Krogman's website. Plus, you can find more stories and sign up for the newsletter at https://rm krogman.com/.

amazon.com/stores/R.-M.-Krogman/author/B0BYPGPWKJ

facebook.com/rmkrogman

instagram.com/r.m.krogman

g   goodreads.com/rmkrogman

WANT MORE OF MIDGATE?

Marked is set in the world of Midgate, where elemental magic flows through people, the bond between man and dragon has been neglected, and the world is divided by the constant fight for power over mankind's head and heart. You will see Davon and Ar'we again.

Set after *Marked*, the epic fantasy *The Keepers of Midgate* follows multiple characters in disparate parts of the world, each on their own journey to right the wrongs they face, and to break free of the bonds of society. As they forge onward, they are drawn to a greater calling, to face and defeat the madness that is tearing their society apart. Check out the first book, *Liberation*, at https://rmkrogman.com/books.

You will see more of Davon in the epic fantasy *The Keepers of Midgate.*

Read More by R. M. Krogman

Keepers of Midgate

Recommended Reading Order

Marked (Novella)

Liberation

Myrmaiden (Novella)

Sundering

Desert Rose

Schism

Phantom: The Chronicles of Thordrin (Novella)

Stand-alone Short Stories (No Order)

The Sun Thief

Whisperer

Gatekeeper

Chronological Reading Order
The Sun Thief
Gatekeeper
Marked (Novella)
Myrmaiden (Novella)
Phantom: The Chronicles of Thordrin (Novella)
Whisperer
Liberation
Desert Rose
Sundering
Schism

About the Author

Rebecca M. Krogman is an epic and dark fantasy author from Iowa, USA.

Her debut novel, *Liberation*, is the first volume of a larger story set in Midgate, a medieval-inspired world of magic, mermaids, and wyverns. She has been developing the *Keepers of Midgate* epic since she was in high school. The main storyline has changed little since then, only gaining more clarity and detail as the characters take on a life of their own. The world has grown in its depth of history, culture, and geography, spawning numerous side stories, prequels, and a sequel.

She loves nature, art, and food, which all funnel into her world-building. Her story's settings span two continents and the sea between, encompassing a diversity of peoples, cultures, and creatures. She is working on a collection of recipes from Midgate, and she loves drawing scenes and characters from the books (although those sketches may never see the light of day). She will never apologize for describing a tree, as she finds trees to be fascinating and far more alive than they get credit for.

When she's not writing about Midgate, she's penning fairy tale retellings. She enjoys mixing familiar pieces from many tales together and may one day reveal to you her *Tinderbox Princess* series.